A Polished Arrow

By

L. Anna Marie Nemitz

PublishAmerica
Baltimore

First printing

ISBN: 1-4137-2942-8
PUBLISHED BY PUBLISHAMERICA, LLLP
www.publishamerica.com
Baltimore

Printed in the United States of America

Dedication

This work is dedicated to the memory of my parents, Carl and Caroline Nemitz; to the memory of my brother Albert, and to the rest of my siblings, Helen, Carl, Dave and Millie. Also, it is an inscription to my Grandparents, Aunts, Uncles and cousins, on the maternal side of my ancestry.

Oct. 2004
To Millie
Best Wishes!
Lorna Marie Nemitz

Acknowledgments

In deepest reverence and awe I again bring to God my praise and thanks for this finished manuscript. It is He that created in me the desire to write. He keeps me focused on my work, and it is He that delivers words to my mind when my mental resourcefulness becomes momentarily feeble. To Him I owe the greatest thanks!

To all the rest who have supplied me with material and other benefits, I am very grateful and deeply moved! God be praised for all of you!

"He made me a polished arrow,
in his quiver he hid me away.
And he said to me, 'You are my servant.'"

—Isaiah: 49: 2b-3a

Chapter One

Strains of Johann Pachelbel's, "Canon In D," melodiously wafted through the air, entering the ear canals of Paul Edgar Riech. He had just opened the door to St. Peter's Lutheran church, an older church nearing its 65th anniversary.

A graduating member of the seminary in St. Louis, Missouri, just weeks before, this was his first day at St. Peter's. He was a tall, clean-shaven, unpretentious man. His thick, sandy, curly hair was well-groomed. Listening for a moment, he then continued on to his study. Closing the door quietly, he sat down at his desk and bowed his head in prayer.

He was a bit apprehensive about this post, questioning if the congregation would readily accept the sermons he rendered. One thing he was positive about—he would not mince any words, telling it as it was written in the Good Book. The Word needed to be proclaimed as it was written, not shaving off a little bit here and a little bit there, so that one might tickle the ears of the beholder. No, he'd stick to his morals and tell it like it was printed. Opening his notebook, he studiously worked on his sermon, the first that he would present to this congregation.

Organized by a small group of people, St. Peter's main nationality was German. True to the nature of the Germans, some were very stubborn.

Paul's heritage was linked with Germany, also, except that around 1870 his great grandfather had married a Chetek Indian maiden. His high cheekbones attested to his Indian lineage.

Living alone in the parsonage, which was near the church, he could lose himself in its many rooms. The white, two-story building was as old as the church. It was quite spacious boasting of five bedrooms, enabling its tenants to rear large families. Some of the church ladies had scrubbed, painted and thoroughly cleaned the parsonage several days before Reverend Riech had moved in from his mother's home in Milwaukee. Paul had decided to use only the bottom floor. Housework was no stranger to him as he had often helped his mother with the housework. It was she that had worked hard to get him through college and seminary. Paul showed his gratitude by helping her with tasks about the house whenever his schedule would allow. His father was deceased.

The church grounds, as well as the regions around, were flat. One could see a mile or more in any direction. Trees were plentiful which added to the beauty of this Minnesota countryside. St. Peter's was situated in the country four miles from Anderville and about ten miles from Spruce Island. Fond memories of this church were tucked away in Tamar's heart. She loved this old country church, the church where she had been confirmed.

This pleasant Friday morning in July, soft breezes blowing, Tamar Niedlich continued practicing the music for Sunday's service. The Reverend Muller, from Minneapolis, had mailed her the hymns for the installation of Reverend Riech the coming Sunday. The esteemed Reverend Muller would be conducting the service.

Tamar, almost nineteen years old, which was rather young for a church organist, had been the organist since she was sixteen. She lived with her parents, brothers and sisters in Anderville, near the outskirts of town. Her light brown, shoulder-length hair was curled about her face, her body attired in a white blouse and navy blue skirt. She had arrived early to practice before the heat of the day fell upon her. She also worked at the pharmacy in Anderville, her work hour starting at 10:00.

The family car was at her disposal for driving to church to practice. However, since the starting of the war, gas was rationed, and most of the time she either had to ride her brother John's bike or practice on the family's old pump organ. The old organ, a remnant from another church, a congregation that had upgraded to an electric organ. Her father had paid for it with a five dollar bill.

This was the year of the Lord, 1945. The nation stood in shock when

President F. D. Roosevelt's demise on April 12th, reached the news arena. Vice President Harry Truman was sworn in as President of the United States. World War II was still in progress, but the Allies were steadily gaining ground. Victory over Europe had already taken place on May 8th. Tamar remembered that day with gratitude, the day when the church bells all rang, at St. Peter's as well as the other churches in the surrounding area, the day of victory for America. St. Peter's held a service that evening, people joyfully thanking God that America was still secure in her freedom. Tamar's Uncle Rufus was still in Germany where he had been fighting to down the Nazi communistic regime. Just six years older than she, her hope was that soon he would be coming home.

Tamar's father worked in the creamery. Their home was near her father's work site making it convenient for him to walk to work. The Niedlich's two-story white dwelling was spacious. Close to the kitchen window, a rose bush offered a sweet aroma to the house whenever the kitchen window was open. The closed-in porch attached to the back of the house, provided a bit more space. A kerosene stove positioned on the porch, which was used for canning and some baking, proved useful and also allowed the kitchen to remain cooler in the summertime.

Tamar's brother, Robert, a year older than she, had just been drafted into the army and was stationed in Texas. A sister, they called Tootie, was sixteen years old; brother John, next in line, was fifteen; her brother Eugene was ten years old; and Ruth, the baby of the family, was four.

Carl and Sophia Platz, Tamar's maternal grandparents, lived in an apartment in Anderville. Dorthea, her mother's younger sister, her husband Bill Beck and their four-year-old daughter, Dorene, lived on a farm a mile outside of Anderville.

Tamar finished her practicing, picked up her music and drove the eight-year-old Ford home, went into the house to drop off her music.

"How did practice go?" her mother asked.

"It went okay. I didn't get to talk to Reverend Riech. I heard him come in while I was practicing. He probably didn't want to interrupt my playing."

"Were any of the ladies there to setup for Sunday's potluck?"

"Not while I was there."

"Perhaps they'll go early Sunday morning to do that. I'm going to bake some apple and lemon pies tomorrow for the potluck. I'll make extra for Reverend Riech. Living alone, I'm sure that he'll appreciate anything that the women of the church can do for him."

"I'm sure that's true. I'm surprised that the church voted in a single man."

"He comes well qualified. Perhaps he's dedicating his entire life to God and feels that a family would be a hindrance."

"That's a possibility. Well I better get to work. See you at supper time."

Tamar left and walked to her place of work.

That afternoon, Maxine, a young woman a bit older than Tamar, and one of the eligible of the congregation, stopped at the drug store for a cool fountain drink. Tamar waited on her.

"Have you had a chance to talk to our new Reverend yet?" she asked.

"I went to practice this morning, but I didn't get to talk to him."

"He sure is good looking. I imagine that all of the unattached young ladies, and probably some that are attached, will be flocking to his doorstep."

"Yes, he is good looking. Perhaps he already has someone special—you know, someone from his home town."

"It's probable, but that won't stop the surge of women to his doorstep."

"Well, some will probably be throwing themselves at him, I suppose. After all, we're only human and who knows how the available will act."

"I'm going to take him a loaf of bread from the batch I made this morning, along with some strawberry jam I made this summer."

"I'm sure he'll appreciate that, Maxine," Tamar answered her.

"Well, I better get over to Reverend Riech's with my offering."

Tamar wished her well and then hurried off to wait on another customer, wondering if Maxine would be one of the host of eligible flocking to Reverend Riech's door.

Maxine Schmit left heading the family car toward the church.

An ample porch attached to the parsonage skirted the full width of the house. Paul happened to be out sweeping it when Maxine drove in. A porch swing attached to the ceiling, was at one end. Two wicker chairs,

with nice padded pillows which his mother had made for him, were placed near by.

"Hi there!" Maxine verbalized as she walked toward the house.

"Hello," Paul answered.

Maxine, handing him her offering, said, "I'm Maxine Schmit and I wanted to bring you some bread that I baked this morning. And jam I made last month. Without a wife to do those things for you, I thought you might enjoy some homemade food."

"I thank you, Maxine. I do appreciate your gift."

He took the items from her and then said, "Have a chair while I take these inside."

Maxine seated herself on the chair he motioned toward and waited for his return. When Paul returned he sat on the swing, which also had a padded seat to match the chairs, and placed one foot across the seat, the other on the floor.

"Tell me about your family, Maxine," he voiced.

Maxine, a buxom five-foot five-inch, dark haired beauty, went on to tell him that she lived with her parents and younger brother and sister on a farm toward Spruce Island. She had intentions of becoming a beautician. A recent graduate from high school, she was planning on going to beauty school in the fall.

"That's an honorable profession. I'm sure that you could do well in that field," he opined. "I see that you do have a direction and that is admirable."

After relating things about the rest of the family, Maxine, hesitating, questioned in which way to direct her conversation. Finally she said, "I best get home to help with the chores. I'll see you on Sunday."

"God willing, you surely will."

Saturday morning the cleaning and baking were in full swing at the Niedlich home. Herb, Tamar's father, had already walked to work when Tamar entered the kitchen. His work started early in the day.

The two boys went out to feed their rabbits and the family dog, Buster. With that chore completed, they raced indoors to ask permission to ride their bikes to Uncle Bill and Aunt Dorthea's. Amanda, Tamar's mother,

allowed it sensing that it was a good place for them. Bill would put them to work, keeping them out of trouble. That left Amanda, Tootie and Tamar to do the cleaning and baking. Amanda checked in on Ruth. Noticing that Ruth was busy playing with her dolls, she commenced with the baking of pies. Tamar mixed the bread dough, setting aside some of the dough to fry for lunch. Tootie saw to the upstairs cleaning; Amanda and Tamar did the downstairs after the baking was completed.

Saturday evening Bill, Dorthea, Dorene and the grandparents, gathered at Herb and Amanda's home. These were great times of sharing for all and became a Saturday night ritual. Ruth, after she had hugged her grandparents, aunt and uncle, took Dorene to her bedroom to play house with her dolls. Tootie and Tamar took turns at the organ, pumping out tunes of their day, like, "Coming In On a Wing and a Prayer," "Bell Bottom Trousers," and "For Me and My Gal," which was a favorite of Tootie and Tamar. They often sang it together. They ended up singing songs from the Lutheran Hymnal. To top off the evening, Tamar helped Amanda make sandwiches and coffee.

Bill was a humorous sort and had the ability to make people laugh. Dorthea, short in stature but not in personality, had a laugh that generated others to laugh. The house seemed to roar with laughter, lifting the roof with its contagious enthusiasm whenever Bill and Dorthea were in their midst. Tamar reveled in the Saturday night get-togethers.

At times they would end up at the grandparents' home but usually, because the Niedlich's had the organ, they rallied around at their home. Bill and Dorthea came into town on Saturday nights to pick up their weekly groceries. Often through the week the Niedlichs would surface at the Beck home, especially during haying season. Dorthea always seemed to be caught short-handed, various tasks always needing attention. She was immensely grateful for the extra helping hands.

As they were eating the braunschweiger sandwiches, along with some of Grandma Sophia's dill pickles, Bill asked Amanda, "Are you taking some rabbit for the pot-luck tomorrow?"

Carl, Amanda's father, a slight, plump, bald-headed man, in his raspy voice said, "If you do please let me know which dish is yours. I'm not going to eat rabbit—never have and never will."

"You don't know what you're missing," Herb replied.

"Don't worry, Pa," Amanda voiced, "There will be no roast rabbit from our pens. You really should try it sometime though, it's just as good as chicken."

"I'll take chicken anytime." Puffing away on his pipe, Carl was very firm about that.

Prompted by Herb, the Niedlich boys had started raising rabbits several years before. It gave them chores to do, developing sound characteristic qualities and responsibilities in them. Their work ethics when they reached manhood would be enhanced, was Herb's thinking. Also, with meat being a shortage due to the war, it was an added bonus to the family to have their own supply of meat. Quite often Amanda prepared Hasenpfeffer, one of the families favorite meals. Obtaining a buyer for rabbit hides, Herb had taught Robert and John how to skin the rabbits and stretch their hides. The boys willingly took to this assignment, considering the fact that it provided spending money for them. With Robert's absence, Eugene was learning the art.

After their guests had left, Herb put his arm around Amanda's shoulder and said, "You know what we should do? Fix rabbit for supper and invite Bill, Dorthea and your folks and not tell your father what it is. I'll wager that he'd eat it."

"I'm sure he would. We can do that." Letting that statement hang for a moment, she finished with, "Maybe we could invite the new minister too. He most likely would appreciate a good meal."

"Why don't we do that?"

"Let's do that next Saturday evening."

Tamar, realizing that Reverend Riech had obligations for that day said, "Mom, there's a youth group meeting next Saturday night. I doubt that he would come."

"Oh...Okay, we can set it up for the next Saturday."

That decision held.

Sunday morning found the Saturday night entertainers getting ready to attend the service at St. Peter's. This was the day to pay homage to the King of their lives, to thank Him for all of His blessings. On this particular

Sunday in July, Paul was to be installed. Tamar had taken extra care in getting ready for this special day, this day when they had a guest speaker. Her hair neatly combed, shoes shined to perfection, she picked out a white rayon dress with cap sleeves that her mother had made for her. Material was hard to come by in this war pressed medium that they were living in. But Tamar felt extremely privileged when her Aunt Dorthea had given the material to her for a birthday gift the year before. Moving toward the stairs, Tamar first checked in the large mirror to make sure her red hat was tilted to her liking, her dress properly buttoned, red belt adjusted correctly, hair in place, lipstick not smeared, and rayon stocking seams straight. Her five-foot, seven-inch slender frame would pass, she reckoned.

The family always left in plenty of time to enable Tamar to get to the pipe organ to limber up her feet and fingers before church began.

As Amanda took the two pies to the parsonage for Reverend Riech, Tamar hurried to the organ to practice. On this special morning Paul Riech was already in his study.

Tamar felt that soon Reverend Muller would be arriving. Seating herself at the organ she fingered through the hymns for the day, going through the liturgy as well.

Placing the prelude in front of her, she judged that it was about time for the service to begin. Glancing in the mirror above the organ, the ushers were signaling her to proceed. With great confidence she touched the keys, giving Johann Pachelbel's "Canon In D" an electrifying rendition. She played as if she were playing for Jesus.

After the service concluded, the women of the church hurried to lay out the food for the potluck. Tamar had a moment to visit with several members. One of the women of the church, with a woman in tow that Tamar didn't recognize, walked to Tamar and introduced her.

"This is Mrs. Riech, Reverend Riech's mother," she said. Tamar greeted her warmly. They exchanged some pleasantries of the day.

Tamar left to help the ladies with the potluck setup. Amanda had brought an apple and a lemon meringue pie, some butter that Amanda had churned, dinner rolls that Tamar had baked and a roast beef. Sophia's offering was a three layer chocolate cake, with seven-minute frosting.

Dorthea came with two different kinds of salad and a pork roast. Although this wasn't a massive congregation, just 126 communicant members, and although there were items rationed due to the war, the tables were well laden with food.

Some of the men folk extended their greetings to Reverend Muller while others welcomed and wished Reverend Riech a blessed union with the congregation at St. Peter's.

Tamar had noticed that some of the young ladies were gathered about Paul. Realizing that as the church organist she would have ample time to talk with him sometime during the week, she proceeded to help the ladies with the food preparation.

Later, after the cleanup had been completed, Paul found a moment when he wasn't surrounded by members, to walk to the kitchen to thank the ladies for the wonderful meal.

Tamar, standing near the sink, was listening to her mother's conversation with their neighbor, Mrs. Ruals.

"My most heartfelt thanks to you ladies for that wonderful meal," Paul voiced.

"You're so very welcome," Maxine's mother replied. " We're so thankful to have you amongst us."

Some of the other women offered their sentiments as well.

Casually ambling to the sink, he took a glass from the cupboard to get himself a drink of water. Looking at Tamar he said, "Thank you for that fine performance this morning."

"It's what I do for my Lord," she joyfully voiced.

"I'm sure that the angels in Heaven sang with you," he responded.

"How soon would you like the hymns for next Sunday? I have them picked out if you would like them now," he went on.

"That would be fine. I really don't need them until Thursday, though."

"Why don't you come along to the office with me and I can give them to you now."

Tamar followed him.

Leaving the door to the office open, he ruffled through the papers on his desk looking for the list of hymns. Wanting to get better acquainted with Tamar, he asked about her family. Relaying to him her fathers

occupation and pertinent items about the rest of the family, Paul then said, "My, what a nice sized family. I have an older sister and often wished that I had a brother. My sister is six years older than I, which kept us from being great pals. She was like a second mother to me. Esther, that's my sister, wanted to be here today, but she lives in Texas where her husband is stationed. He's a chaplain in the army. With her young ones it would have been a strain on her to come alone with them for this special day. They have a cute three-year-old girl and twin boys a year old."

"I'd say that she does have her hands full. I did get to meet your mother. She's a very lovely lady," Tamar offered.

Just then, Maxine dressed in a blue cotton print dress with a square neck trimmed with lace; darts sewn in just the right places on the bodice to show off her bounty, stood at the door. Talking to Paul she said, "Oh here you are. Some of the young people are getting a ball game together. They wanted to know if you'd like to play?"

"Yes I would. Thank you for inviting me."

He handed Tamar the list of hymns and thanked her again. Tamar left to sit with the younger generation. They were going to watch the ball game. Maxine, too, wanted to get in on the action. She took her stance, making her mark for the day as catcher.

Nearing 4:00 people started loading up their vehicles, the farmers needing to get home to their chores.

Amanda suggested that Bill and Dorthea return after chores to the Niedlich home, and they would have their own potluck from their leftover food. They agreed.

On Monday morning Paul took his mother to the bus depot. She had a job to get to on Tuesday morning. Hugging her and wishing her a safe journey, he reverberated, "I'll pray you into God's keeping, and with His willingness, I'll see you at Thanksgiving." He kissed her cheek.

Chapter Two

On Sunday, July 15th, Reverend Paul Riech gave his first sermon at St. Peter's. The church was packed leaving little room for people to move about in the back. Some additional seating had to be set up. The driving attraction was the fact that most were curious about Reverend Riech's first performance at St. Peter's. The war also, brought many to the church and to their knees.

Tamar, seated at the organ, was playing the hymn, "By Grace I'm Saved, Grace Free and Boundless." Reverend Riech, clothed in his black robe with a white clerical collar, entered the pulpit during the singing of the last verse and bowed his head in prayer.

The hymn ended. Tamar, wanting stronger concentration powers as Paul pressed on with his sermon, moved to a chair which had been placed beside the organ.

Reverend Riech, lifting his head from his prayerful mode, motioned the congregation to rise. Reading the scripture from the 15th chapter of Luke, starting with the 11th verse, he read St. Luke's account of the prodigal son. After the reading he signaled them to be seated.

"Peace be unto you from our Lord and Savior Jesus Christ," he began. "From our Father's throne above to our dwelling here below, comes this divine message that I have just read for you. It is a message that should cheer the hearts of all of us gathered here this morning. This parable that Jesus was attempting to get across to the Jewish religious leaders and the authorities on Jewish law, is one that should also have a great impact on our lives."

Scanning his eyes over the congregation, then looking down at his Bible, lifting his eyes again to the congeners, he eloquently illuminated his

deliberation on the prodigal son. The story unfolded: the younger son requested his inheritance from his father. His father certainly was disappointed but did grant him his inheritance. Going to a distant land, and girdling himself with prostitutes, drunkenness and unrighteous living, he squandered all of his money.

The windows and doors of the church were all open, leaving in the little air that moved about. Ceiling fans were operating at full speed. A baby in the audience started to fuss. Paul talked louder. The mother of the baby wanting to hear the sermon, reluctantly gave in and took her child to the basement. Paul readjusted his voice. Tamar noticed that he had captivated the attention of his entire audience. They hung on to every word that he uttered.

Reverend Riech went on with the story, relating how the prodigal found himself without money when a great famine swept over the land. "He is near starvation and persuades a farmer to hire him to feed his pigs. The young man became very hungry. No one gave him anything to eat. He associates with the swine in their filthy habitat. The pods that the pigs were eating looked enormously appealing to him. Finally, coming to his senses he thought, *At home even the hired hands have food enough with even food to spare. Here I am dying of hunger. I will go home to my Father and say, 'Father I have sinned against both heaven and you and am no longer worthy of being called your son. Please take me on as a hired hand.'*" The prodigal returns to his father.

"Now comes the significant descry of this entire parable," Paul discloses. "Having squandered all of his inheritance the road home wasn't so easy. The long walk back home was made even more difficult by a stomach that cried out for food. Still he was determined to go to his father. While he was yet a far distance away, the father notices his wayward son returning to him and has compassion and loving pity on him. He runs to meet him. He not only embraces him but he kisses him! Reflect on that for a moment if you will. Here is his son who reeks of pigs and squalor. What does his father do? He kisses him!"

Reverend Riech brings the lesson home. "Fellow Christians, we too, are prone to eat from Satan's table, wallowing around in his muck and filth. But there is good news. Regardless of the circumstance we unfortunately find ourselves caught up in, we have this lesson to rely on.

Concerned that our sins are as filthy as pigs, our Heavenly Father only desires us to return to Him. He isn't affected by the smell of swine. No, His only fervor is that we come to Him in repentance. In a repentance where our stains can be washed away in the blood of the lamb. What a loving, compassionate Father we have! God has no pleasure in seeking our death and ruination. He patiently waits for us to return to him. Yes, he patiently waits for us. Sometimes we're so caught up in our sin that we can't see the forest for the trees. But He'll be there to welcome us home. With open arms He will receive us; yes, he'll even kiss us. Dear Friends, now is the time to make things right between you and your God. We do not know when we'll breathe our last breath.

"Our compassionate Savior seeks nothing more than the willingness of our hearts to walk in His ways. If we say that we love Him then out of love for Him we should strive to ungrudgingly give of our best for Jesus: giving Him our talents, telling others about this wonderful God that we serve, helping those who are less fortunate than we are—in doing so we are doing it as if we were doing it for Jesus. Spending time in His Word with Him is well pleasing to Him. May we all attain to His higher calling."

Paul brought the sermon to a close and left the pulpit. Tamar played the last hymn. Pronouncing the benediction over his flock, the Three-Fold-Amen was sung and Paul walked to the back of the church to greet the congregation. Tamar quickly shifted her music to the postlude and played on.

Starting at the front row, the ushers dismissed the people. When Maxine and her family, seated imposingly near the front, reached Pastor Riech, Gloria, Maxine's mother, reached for his hand and said, "What a wonderful message."

Paul said, "Yes, Jesus left this world, leaving behind words of wisdom, hope and peace for all of us."

"He certainly did." Then altering the mode of her conversation she continued with, "We'd love to have you come for dinner, that is, if no one else has invited you?"

"Thank you for the thoughtful invitation. Yes, I'd love to. We can become better acquainted, too, as we dine."

Gloria went on to give him directions. They hurried on home to finish

up the preparations.

As Herb, clutching little Ruth's hand, and Amanda went through the receiving line, they too, remarked on his wonderful message. Inviting him to supper for the coming Saturday night, he readily accepted their invitation.

Tamar was the last one to shake his hand. His hand felt warm and solid, strong and large. It engulfed her much smaller hand.

"God's blessings, Tamar," he said.

"His blessings be with you, too. You are right, Reverend Riech, what a wonderful God we have. Thank you for bringing us that discerning message."

"You're welcome. We all need to be renewed daily in our faith. I'll be coming into town sometime this week. Would you like me to drop the list of hymns at your home?"

"You can do that or leave the list at the drug store if you'd like."

"Good. I'll see you sometime this week then."

Paul decided against wearing his suit jacket but had on a tie. Climbing into his 1937 Ford, he sweltered with the heat it radiated. Rolling down the front windows he proceeded to drive the few miles to the Schmit home. The momentum of the car effectuated a small amount of moving air. He noticed the fields with their ripening grain. Soon it would be time for the harvest. *Yes,* he thought, *This is a good reminder that God's harvest will happen one day. There's much work to be done. I hope that I can reach all of the people that are entrusted to my care, encouraging them to be ready for the great harvest.*

Arriving at the Schmit's home, Phillip, Maxine's brother, and next to her in age, was waiting on the porch for Reverend Riech. He strolled to the car to meet him and ushered him to the house. Gloria met him at the door, leading him to the living room where Fred, her husband, was reading the Sunday paper.

"Come in, come in," he said as he stood to receive his firm hand shake. "This chair here is fairly comfortable. Just make yourself at home."

They were both seated and Reverend Riech started with, "The crops look unquestionably good and healthy."

"Yes, providing no hail hits we should have a good harvest." Waiting

a few seconds, Fred then continued with, "So you hale from Milwaukee?"

"Yes, I do. I was raised there. My father was a butcher. He passed away when I was fifteen."

"So you decided not to follow in your father's footsteps?"

"When my father died it left me with a big emptiness. Our minister was sensitive to my needs and counseled me a lot. I spent some time with him. It was than that I decided to become a servant of the Lord."

The conversation went on.

Soon they were called to the dinner table. Maxine was seated across from Paul. Surmising that Paul had a bona fide "in" with God, Fred requested his expertise in offering the blessing.

Dishes of mouth watering food were passed, first to the guest then to the rest of the family. Maxine had an eye on Paul, paying attention that it wasn't noticeable. "Your sermon was excellent this morning," she said.

"I thank you, Maxine. I get a lot of help from above," he replied.

"Do you think that really happened—about the younger son, I mean?" she asked.

"That was just one of Jesus' many fables, if you will, that he told with its purposeful intention. Allegory might be a better word than fable."

"I like that story," Phillip acknowledged.

"It is a wonderful story, Phillip."

After a few silent moments Maxine inquired of Paul, "What do you do for entertainment?"

"I like to fish. Wisconsin was a great place for that. I was equally delighted when I was able to obtain a position in Minnesota. I'm sure that the fishing will be just as good here as in Wisconsin."

"You're right," Fred said. "There are lots of lakes around, some in walking distance."

"I'll scout around and I'm sure that I'll find them."

"You don't have to look far. The Becks, I'm sure that you have already met them, have a lake adjacent to their property."

"Good. I'll have to call on them soon and ask permission to fish."

"They are related to the organist," Maxine stated.

"Oh, I didn't know that. I haven't had a chance to talk with Tamar at great length yet."

So the afternoon went. Paul showing great interest in their farming operation and in the conversation.

When it was time for chores Gloria invited Paul to stay for supper.

"I'd love to. Maybe I should have dressed for farm work," he remarked.

"We have plenty of help," Fred said. "You're welcomed to observe though, if you'd like."

"I'll do that," he replied. His aim was to get in touch with the farming community. In his Sunday-go-to-meeting clothes Paul wandered out to look over their operation. He was impressed. The farm yard was nice and clean. He thought, *This is a good lesson for a city dweller. From now on I'll be prepared when I'm asked for dinner out in the country. I'll dress accordingly.*

The evening went on, Maxine asking Paul questions and getting quite familiar with him. Fred and Gloria, too, joined in the conversation. Phillip occasionally got the floor and asked him about sports. Paul allowed that he had played basketball in high school. That prompted a good opening for Maxine since she, too, had played basketball. Geraldine, the youngest member of the family, thirteen years old, was a bit shy. However, Paul did inspire her to join in by asking her about school.

When she revealed the class that she would be going into, Paul remarked, "You'll be in my confirmation class then next year."

"She will be. Phillip will be in your class this fall," Gloria replied.

Paul thought, *I see why she's so bashful. The others talk for her.*

Concurrently at the Niedlich home, John sought out his friend, Bobby, that afternoon. They were in the same class at school and had been trusted friends since the Niedlich family had moved into the area five years before. Eugene wanted to go along and was disappointed when John refused to take him.

Amanda said, "One day you'll have a friend to discuss things with, too, Eugene. Just be patient."

"But I don't have anything to do, Mom."

"Why don't you play with Buster. He's been tied up all day. It would be good for him to get some exercise."

Their property included a half acre of ground, ensuring space for

Buster to roam about. Herb had intentions of fencing the property, albeit the war made it impossible for the citizens to buy the commodities they needed, like fencing material.

Amanda knew that Eugene was of good temperament and that he would find some way to entertain himself. She often regretted the five year difference between the two boys, too many years to be great pals.

When it was time for their supper, John, along with his buddy, Bobby, had returned home. John asked his mother if Bobby could stay for supper. Always willing to accommodate the friends of her children, Amanda said, "Bobby we have set an extra plate for you to stay for supper."

Bobby offered Amanda his thanks.

After supper, a game of softball appeared to be the delight of the two pals. Other players were needed, too. Eugene was invited to play with them. John persuaded Tootie into playing, also. They still needed other players and Herb offered to play with them. Ruth went out, too, and chased after balls.

Amanda got out her crocheting and Tamar decided to take a walk, walking to the main part of town.

There was a café open and Tamar opted for a cool drink. The town was rather quiet. War time had taken most of the eligible suitors so Tamar didn't date much. Sunday afternoons and evenings seemed to be down times for her, especially after the merriment she experienced on Saturday evenings. Her thoughts turned to college. She had been accepted at Concordia College, in St. Paul, Minnesota. She would be leaving in August. Deep into her thoughts, they were interrupted when a classmate sat down beside her. Rose, a bit shorter than Tamar, with blond hair and not uncomely, said, "Hi Tamar. What's going on?"

"Hi Rose. Just trying to pass the time. What are you up to?"

"I was wanting to go to the movies. It's too warm for that, though."

They chatted about their school, where they were going with their lives and anything that pertained to the times.

Tamar said, "I want to get some sewing done for college."

"That will be a trick with material so scarce."

"Mom and Aunt Dorthea are planning on going to Hutchinson soon

to see if there is any available."

"Well, good luck."

"What are you going to do now that school is over?" Tamar asked.

"Well, I'm not sure yet. I'll probably try to pick up a job, maybe a waitress job."

"With the war news as it is maybe our young men will be coming home soon. Maybe you'll get married?"

"I hope that you are right about the young men coming home. I'm not sure that I want to get married yet."

Soon the darkness crept into their surroundings. Tamar decided that it was time to return home.

Amanda had a large garden which, for the most part, had already been harvested.

There were still a few items to contend with, potatoes to be dug, heads of cabbage to be made into sauerkraut. The earlier tomatoes had been picked and canned but there were still more coming on.

John and his friend, Bobby, were sitting in the dark on the back steps, Buster, the German Shepherd, beside them. Buster was a playful dog, just nine months old. However, he was showing signs of being a good watch dog.

Several neighborhood, mischievous youngsters were out prowling in the darkened night. John said, "Shhh…I hear something." Buster perked up his ears. John took hold of his collar. The boys were very quiet. Soon a few heads appeared in the garden. John could see that they were picking tomatoes, probably to throw at someone. He let go of Buster's collar. Buster bounded for the boys. A lot of shrieking broke the stillness. The mischievous boys high-tailed it to safer corners. John and Bobby, seized with mirth, punched one another in the arm as they went to retrieve Buster, tying him to his dog house.

Herb stepped out to see what the ruckus was about. When the boys told him of the tomato conspiracy, Herb said, "Good dog!" He cautioned John that they'd have to exercise training so that Buster wouldn't bite anyone. "We don't want a law suit on our hands." Walking over to Buster he petted him saying, "You keep those boys out of our garden."

Chapter Three

Monday was Paul's day off. Starting his morning with food for his soul first, he read a chapter from the book of Jeremiah. After his prayerful time with God he went to fix his breakfast of bacon, eggs and toast. The coffee pot was always on, relying on that stimulant to revive him whenever he felt weary.

Breakfast over with, dishes washed, he engaged his entire being into cleaning the house. He had already done his laundry on Saturday. The first floor of the parsonage consisted of a good sized master bedroom, a smaller bedroom, bathroom, dinning room, living room, kitchen and back porch. As one entered the front door into the vestibule, off to the left was Paul's study. There was a basement that housed the washing machine and wash tubs. Sturdy clothes lines were in the backyard with some additional lines strung across the basement walls to adapt when rainy days occurred.

Dressed in a polo shirt and dungarees, Paul, busy cleaning the kitchen, heard a knock at the door. Setting aside the mop, he went to answer it. *Who might that be on a Monday morning?* he thought. *I hope that it isn't bad news.*

Opening the front door he faced a man of medium stature, wearing a pair of striped bib overalls that had seen many washings. A denim cap covered his graying hair.

"Good morning, Reverend," he uttered. "I brought you a casserole that the Mrs. made for you."

"Why thank you, Mr. Weise. Please thank Mrs. Weise for me also. Would you like to come in?"

"Well, I probably have a few minutes to spare."

With that said, Paul ushered him into the living room. The living room contained odds and ends of furniture, some that were given to him and some that he had purchased. There was a wine colored sofa and two easy chairs, one matched the sofa and the other was royal blue. Carpeting, that had just been vacuumed, blended well. It had a dark blue background with flowers of various colors, some of the flowers picking up the wine color of the sofa and chair. Several end tables with lamps on them were beside the two chairs and sofa.

Ernst Weise was part owner of the lumber company in town. His right leg had been amputated years ago due to a motorcycle accident. Walking with a slight limp, it didn't deter him from earning a good living. His wife, Ilsa, had come from Germany to marry Ernst almost twenty years ago. They had three children, Ronald, who was a senior in high school, Florence, a freshman and Genevieve, in seventh grade.

Ernst seated himself on the royal blue overstuffed chair, his wooden leg positioned rigidly in front of him.

After conversing about the weather, Ernst's livelihood, and a few other pertinent items, Ernst offered, "My father's brother, Frederich, was a preacher at this church once."

"Is that a fact?"

"Ya, that's so. He preached here for six years."

"I don't know much about the history of this church. When did he have his ministry here?"

"He was here before our last preacher. People were always making up stories about him. I know that they aren't true."

"That's a shame. Well, you can be assured that I will strive to conduct myself properly, and I'm sure that your uncle did too. I'd hate to leave this congregation with tales dragging behind me. Where is your uncle now?"

"Oh, he's retired and lives in Mankato. Well, you'll have your hands full keeping your nose clean, with the sort of some that we have living around here."

Visiting for a few minutes longer, Ernst departed leaving Paul to do the rest of his cleaning.

As Paul continued on with his work, the words that Ernst had uttered staggered his mind. Finally he put it to rest and knew that he'd have to rely

heavily on his Heavenly Father in an attempt to keep falsehoods from arising.

On Tuesday, Paul was at his office in the church looking over his schedule for the week. His aim was to visit all of the church members first and then try to visit some of the unchurched. Judging that this would be a good day to start his visitations, he followed his plan. Viewing the list of members, the first on the list was the family of Martin and Laura Abends, their three children, Rose, who graduated with Tamar, her younger brothers, Samuel and Warren. Martin was a High School English teacher. *Ah, what an ideal time to start on my mission. It's vacation time and Martin will probably be home.*

He got into his Ford and headed for town, searching for 205 Elm Street, where the Abends lived. It was 1:30 when he knocked on their door. He looked about the well trimmed lawn as he waited an answer to his knock.

"Well, good afternoon, Reverend Riech," Laura said as she opened the door and shook the extended hand. Inviting him in she offered, "We're in the kitchen drinking coffee. Would you like to join us?"

Paul, feeling right at home obliged and followed her into their sunny kitchen. The kitchen was painted light blue with white criss-cross curtains at the windows. Potted plants seemed to be everywhere. The hardwood parquet floor was waxed and buffed to a fine luster. Martin rose from the table and greeted him, shaking his hand. Paul noticed an open catalog of wallpaper samples on the table.

"It looks like you are busy planning to be busy," Paul verbalized.

"Yes," Martin said, "Laura likes to keep me occupied. She says it keeps me out of trouble." They all laughed.

"He needs to be busy," Laura ventured. "Otherwise he pesters the daylights out of me."

"Now, now. You're telling tales, Laura."

Paul chuckled at them, knowing full well that they were teasing one another. The atmosphere in this home appeared to be homey and happy. He had a good feeling about this couple.

Rose appeared on the scene and blended into the conversation. They

discussed her relaxed attitude of not knowing where to go with her life. College was mentioned but Rose seemed uninterested.

"Maybe in another year," she volunteered.

"Sometimes it's hard to get back into the swing of things after you've been away from studies that long," Paul offered.

"That might be so," she replied, "but I really don't know yet what I want to do. I just want to take off a year and decide."

Thus went the discussion. They talked about the two boys, Samuel and Warren. Samuel was a junior in high school, Warren would be in the seventh grade—another one for Reverend Riech's confirmation class.

Leaving the Abends home, Paul drove to the main part of town, parked his Ford and went into the drug store to drop off the list of hymns for Tamar.

"Hello, Tamar," he said. "I brought the list of hymns for you."

A dialogue went on about the hymns. Noticing that someone was waiting to be assisted, Paul said, "Please wait on your customer. I have time, I can wait."

He found a vacant table and sat down. Finishing with the patron Tamar joined Paul. They finished up the business about the hymns. Aware that there were no customers waiting for Tamar, Paul visited with her for a short while.

"Well, I mustn't keep you. Anyway, I'll see you on Saturday night." He left.

On Wednesday morning Amanda made sure that John and Eugene went to Mrs. Oberling's to do her lawn and get her groceries. She was intent on making reliable young men out of her sons. Mrs. Oberling was arthritic and spent most of her time indoors. After her husband passed away it was very difficult for her to get her groceries, shovel snow and mow her yard. Amanda offered her the help of her boys. Mary Oberling was grateful for the generosity of Amanda and the boys. Often times she would give them treats for their good Samaritan deeds.

Dorthea, a bit behind with her work on this same day, had an idea. Taking Dorene with her, she cranked up the old Model T, drove into

town to see if Tootie would be able to help her out for a few hours.

The Model T was doing double duty for the Becks. It fended for a pickup truck whenever sacks of feed needed to be hauled. The front seat had to be taken out whenever it was doing its other duty.

Arriving at her sister's home, Dorthea opened the door yodeling, "Yoo hoo, is anyone here?" Tootie and Amanda came from upstairs when they heard her voice. Dorthea relayed the reason she was there.

Amanda said, "Tootie's been at a loss for something to do. You rescued her."

On their way to the farm, Dorthea stopped to pick up a few things from the store. Getting back into the car, ready to head for home, Dorene was sitting in the back seat behind the driver. Dorthea started up the car again, backing it up like a well-trained Marine. Then shifting gears, the car started balking and choking like a mad bull. Startled, she saw a pair of legs flying into her peripheral view. Stopping the car, she assessed the ordeal. Making sure that Tootie and Dorene were okay, she then laughed till she cried. "I guess Uncle Bill forgot to tighten down the seat," she said, still laughing and wiping her eyes.

That wasn't the end of the excitement. Laughing away about the incident, she unintentionally pulled on the steering wheel while she was laughing. Almost home, to her horror she found herself with the steering wheel in her hand. Having her wits about her, she stopped the car. Now it was Tootie's turn to laugh at her. With the steering wheel in her hand and in the air, not in a useable position, her aunt posed a hilarious sight. Getting her insight back, Dorthea, too, laughed. She was able to get the wheel back on in some sort of fashion so that they could drive the rest of the way home.

"My, this has sure been a day," Dorthea remarked.

"Well, at least we are all safely here. I sure hope that no one on the street saw my bottom," Tootie replied.

"You were okay, Tootie. Only your feet and legs were showing."

"How will I explain this to my friends that might have been on the sidewalk watching?"

Dorthea didn't answer her, she just laughed some more.

Abundantly blessed with sunshine on Saturday, the Niedlich home was a wave of busyness. Around 4:30, Carl and Sophia walked to their daughter's home with the intention of helping Amanda get things ready.

Carl joined Herb in the living room. A fan, circulating air, provided enough coolness for this event. The war news was the topic of most of their conversation, Carl hoping that his son, Rufus, would soon be coming home.

Soon Bill, Dorthea and Dorene appeared. Dorthea had brought some coleslaw for the meal. They knew about the rabbit caper.

When Paul drove in the driveway Eugene hurried out to meet him. They had their conversation as they walked to the house.

"Come on in," Eugene directed.

Amanda met them and acknowledged Paul's handshake. Ushering Paul to the living room, Herb vacated his chair to shake hands with Paul. Although Herb was considered a tall man, he didn't measure up to Paul. Paul towered over him. Being seated after shaking hands with the rest of the family, conversations ensued; Paul assimilating the order of Carl and Sophia's family.

The meal was ready and Amanda had them seated. Herb offered the blessing. Everyone was eagerly waiting to see if Carl would eat the rabbit. Amanda had dipped the rabbit in beaten eggs, then wrapped it in fine cracker crumbs and baked it with onion. The aroma was tantalizing.

Starting the mashed potatoes around the table, Amanda first handed them to Paul. The gravy came next, then the meat. Everyone's eyes were on Grandpa, except Paul, that is. He was not privy to this prank. Like everyone suspected, Carl did take some meat. The rest of the dishes were passed around and the topic for the most part, was on how Paul was getting accustomed to his new surroundings. Fishing was brought into the conversation. Paul, remembering that Fred Schmit had mentioned that the Beck family had a lake near their property, said, "I hear that you have a lake adjacent to your property, Bill."

"We do have," Bill replied. "You can come out and fish anytime that you want to."

"Thank you very much. I just might do that on my day off Monday. Maybe you would like to go with me, John? You can show me around."

John's thought was that he'd rather go fishing with his buddy, Bobby. He wouldn't have to be on his best going-to-church kind of behavior. He was a bit shy around the intellectual type. But he agreed.

It was time to pass seconds. Everyone noticed that Grandpa took another piece of meat. Carl never said a word. The others complimented Amanda on the fine meal.

The evening passed with talk of relevant subject matter. Reverend Riech, interested in Tamar's education, did get a chance to talk with her more, and was surprised to hear that she would be going away to college. They discussed who would be the organist when she left. "I'm planning on coming home some weekends and will still be able to attend to my function as organist. Tootie actually plays with more ease than I do," Tamar offered.

"Let's hear you play something, Tootie," he suggested.

Tootie got on the organ stool, readjusted the stops and proceeded to play, "Turkey In The Straw."

"She plays that piece better than I do," Tamar asserted

"Let's hear some hymns," was Paul's next request.

She chose, "A Mighty Fortress is Our God," playing it very well. Those that knew the hymn by heart sang along with her, others stood beside her and sang from the hymnal she was using. Paul had a beautiful tenor voice. Bill sang bass, Dorthea sang alto along with Tootie. Tamar and her mother sang soprano. The rest just sang. When that hymn ended they sang another and another.

Paul said, "Well, I should have brought some hymnals along. You've got quite a choir here. We'll have to see about getting a church choir going soon. Tamar, you are a beautiful soprano. Being the church organist we never hear your voice."

Tamar thanked him saying that she was thankful that God had given her that gift.

By this time it was late and Paul excused himself so he could present himself well rested in the morning.

Everyone else prepared to leave. Dorthea, with a, "he ate the rabbit," smile on her face, winked at Amanda. Amanda returned a smile, nodding her head.

Once home, Sophia told Carl that he had eaten rabbit. He said, "I knew it was going to be rabbit all along. I sure did get a good meal out of my daughter by telling her I'd never eat rabbit. The jokes is really on them"

"Well, you never told me that you knew."

"There's just some things that you keep to yourself," Carl answered.

Chapter Four

The closing hymn, "Abide With Us Dear Savior," floated through the open windows of St. Peter's the following morning. The service had gone well, Paul addressing his congregation with the Beatitudes; the nine declarations of blessedness which Jesus gave, called, The Sermon On The Mount. He sent his heartfelt thanks to his Lord.

The Schmit family, again seated near the front, trailed to the back of the church to receive Reverend Riech's handshake.

"Another marvelous sermon," Gloria said.

"God has again increased my understanding and it is to Him that I owe the credit," Paul replied.

"If you haven't been invited for dinner, we'd love for you to come and eat with us."

"Thank you, Mrs. Schmit. I would love to accept your invitation, but I do have other plans for today. Maybe another time."

"Anytime that you feel like a full meal just give a holler. You're always welcome."

He thanked her and continued greeting his flock.

His thought was, not that he wouldn't like going to the Schmit's, but taking into consideration that they had a beautiful daughter, being seen with that family too often could entice people to engage their tongues in groundless rumors. He'd keep himself from wagging tongues if he could help it in anyway. Besides, he had letters to write and Sunday afternoon would be a good time to do that.

Maxine, with her very watchful, beautiful eyes, noticed that Tamar was always last to shake Paul's hand. She wished that she were closer to them

so that she could hear what he was saying to her.

"It was a genuine pleasure to spend an evening with you and your family last evening. We'll all have to get together again for a 'singsperation,'" Paul said to Tamar.

"It was indeed a fun evening. We must try that again before I leave for college."

"I'll definitely allow time for it."

The church emptied and Paul went home and spent the afternoon writing his letters.

What a fine day for fishing, Paul thought as he looked out of the kitchen window on Monday morning. *This will be a great day!* He carried on with his spiritual reinforcement and breakfast. On Sunday morning he had discussed the fishing meet with John and it had been decided that they would walk to the Beck's. Paul felt that the exercise would be good for him. Then too, he would be saving gas for more important traveling, like visiting the shut-ins and the hospitalized.

Taking up his fishing pole and tackle box, he started on his four mile trek to the Niedlich's home. At 8:00 in the morning, the soft, cool breeze was exhilarating. Paul knew that by afternoon when fishing was over, his return trip home would no doubt be very warm.

Meadowlarks were offering their sweet songs as Paul, with his fishing pole slung over his shoulder, whistled a tune as he walked along the road. Mr. Zinndorf, a member of his congregation, happened along in his Model A, pulling over to the side of the road.

"Good morning, Reverend. I see you're going fishing. Can I give you a lift?"

"Thank you Mr. Zinndorf. I was really intending to get some exercise. But thank you for your offer."

"Okay then. I see that you are fishing for fish instead of men today."

"That I am. Just as Jesus did, he rested at times too."

"Well, have a good day fishing."

Paul waved him on and continued his trek into town.

Arriving at the Niedlich's home, Amanda, in a tan dress which had vertical thin lines of green and brown stripes going through it, and

covered with a soft green bibbed apron, met him at the door and bid him to enter, welcoming him into the kitchen. Tamar was at the sink washing the breakfast dishes. He greeted her.

Amanda was a tall person, an inch taller than Tamar, with short, light-brown hair that had a few strands of gray showing. After giving birth to her six children she had put on a few extra pounds, adding a little plumpness to her stature.

"Looks like a fine day for fishing," Tamar volunteered.

"God has allowed us a beautiful day," he replied.

"The coffee pot is still on, could I get you some coffee?"

"Thank you for your offer, but I think I've had more than my share this morning."

"When you return, I'll have lunch on for the two of you," Amanda offered.

"That will be much appreciated Mrs. Niedlich. Fishermen do get hungry."

"Yes, fresh air and the sun shining off of the lake has that affect on people."

"That it does."

John was ready so the two departed.

Trying to get John into a conversation was a challenge. John would answer him but contributed nothing that Paul could get a handle on for additional discourse. Finally Paul asked him about his friend, Bobby. That was the circumspection that he needed. He had entered a subject that John related to. He offered insights that he and Bobby had been involved in at school and things that they had achieved there as well, along with happenings at their leisure time. Paul relaxed, comprehending that now he had a comfortable companion for the day.

Soon they were at the lake, the water shimmering in its blue embellishment. The sky was blue with a few cirrus clouds moving slowly through the heavens, none that looked threatening. John showed him the spot that he liked best.

"You've picked a heavenly spot, John," Paul remarked.

The lake was quite deep at this site, waist deep if one stood at the edge. There was a nice sized rock that John loved to fish from and several trees

for shade.

John offered Paul the rock.

"It's your spot, John. I'll just sit here on the grass and fish. This is just as good. It's an ideal place for me to meditate."

They angled worms onto their hooks and started their fishing incentive. Paul, wearing a fisherman's hat, hands behind his head, laid back on the ground, hat pulled over his eyes in an attempt to meditate for a few minutes. His pole was anchored in the bank of the lake.

In a few minutes John said, "You've got a bite, Reverend." Paul hiked up his hat and gave his pole a jerk. "What do you know? A bullhead," Paul exclaimed.

"Not much for size. It might do for my supper though," he concluded.

They fished on, hooking a few now and then. John was getting to the point where he didn't mind fishing with Paul, since he was a rather quiet fisherman. He didn't have to come up with a lot of small-talk.

The sun coming around toward noon, Paul again was in his meditative mode, hat pulled down but yet able to see his line. Suddenly his fishing pole arched way down, indicating that he had a whopper. He grabbed his pole, slipping and floundering around, trying to grasp for something that would avert his fall. A big splash announced his dip in the lake. Grabbing for his hat and pole, righting himself, Paul found that he was waist deep in the lake. John observing the ordeal, really wanted to laugh but thought better of that idea. He would have if it had been his friend, Bobby.

"What a kettle of fish," Paul remarked. "Not only did I take a bath, I lost my fish as well. Well I guess that ends our fishing for today."

"We can walk over to Aunt Dorthea's. Maybe she has some dry clothes for you," John offered.

"You're forgetting one thing, my friend," he replied, "your Uncle Bill is much shorter than I am."

"That's true. But at least you'd have dry pants on."

The two decided to walk over to the Beck's. Dorthea was in her kitchen cleaning eggs to take to town. Hearing voices she went to the door. Never being one to suppress a laugh, she shook with laughter. "I see that you swam for your fish," she exclaimed.

"The swim would have been worth it if I could have captured the fish,"

he replied.

"Well, come on in. Let's get you some dry clothes."

Paul had long ago ceased to be embarrassed by predicaments. *What's the use of it? Nothing can be done after it has happened,* was his philosophy.

Dorthea brought out a pair of Bill's trousers and a shirt and showed him where he could change. After changing he hung his wet clothes on the clothes line to dry. With Bill's trousers on, pant legs almost to the calves of Paul's legs, he presented quite a sight.

Dorthea wanted to laugh. Going to the pantry, giving the impression that she was getting things for lunch, she gave way to her laughter. Getting it out of her system she returned to the kitchen.

Paul ventured, "Well, I won't win any beauty contest but, at least I'm dry."

Dorthea chuckled and said, "Well, you might win a prize for the best dressed hillbilly."

"You have a good point there."

Dorthea then suggested, "You might as well eat lunch with us."

"Mom was going to have lunch ready for us," John said.

"Well, we'll just crank up the operator and get your mom on the line—let her know that you'll be eating with us."

An hour and a half later Paul and John were on their way home. Paul's clothes had dried sufficiently he felt, rationalizing that the seams could dry on their walk home.

At the Niedlich's home, Amanda invited him to stay for supper.

"I would really love to do that, but I think that I best get home with my fish. I really appreciate your offer, Mrs. Niedlich. Another time for sure." Paul left.

Riding her tricycle down the sidewalk in front of the house, Ruth took notice of her father walking home from work. She got off of her tricycle and ran to meet him. Ruth was fine-boned and small, still able to be picked up and hugged. In his bleached white shirt and pants, Herb lifted her, placed her on his hip and gave her a hug. Talking to her he also reminded her that she must put her tricycle away.

The Niedlich's supper table that evening was filled with conversation

about the preacher's fall into the lake. Amanda complimented John for not laughing at Paul's mishap.

"I really wanted to laugh, Mom. I had a hard time to keep from laughing."

Soon the table talk turned to Loretta, the woman who lived at the end of their block.

"I wonder if the minister knows about the talk going on about her?" John asked.

"You surely didn't mention it John, did you?" Amanda questioned.

"He'll not hear it from me," he answered.

The talk around town was that as soon as Frank, Loretta's husband, left for work, another man entered their home and spent some time there. The town gossips insinuations assailed toward Loretta.

"Anyway," Amanda suggested, "He may have a perfectly innocent reason for stopping at her house."

"But every day, Mom?"

"She's innocent until proven guilty and I'm sure that I'm not going to be the one to find out."

Thus ended that topic for the night.

On Tuesday afternoon there was a knock on Paul's front door. He had just picked up the keys to his Ford.

Opening the door, Maxine was on the other side, giving him her prettiest smile, white, even teeth showing. "Hi there! Mother sent me over with some meat loaf. She made some for us for supper and made extra for you."

"Thank you, Maxine for bringing it over. Please thank your mother for me. I do appreciate you folks' generosity."

He took the gift from her and said, "I was just on my way to visit Mrs. Oberling, otherwise I would ask you to visit for a bit. Thank you again."

"You are very welcome," Maxine said. She was a mite disappointed, hoping that he would have time to chat with her for awhile.

Chapter Five

Setting aside Wednesdays for visitations, Paul, in his church study, was glancing over the list of members. He had been introduced to a host of members on his first three Sundays at St. Peter's. Surveying the list, it contained the names of several members who appeared at church only on high volume Sundays, such as Easter and Christmas. Knowing that they, too, needed to be reached, for this day he decided on people that were regular attendees.

Retaining the match of faces to names was a giant test for him. The A's he had already conquered. Looking at the members in the B category, there was a Boling, a face he couldn't come up with. Braun, next on the list, he had an inclination regarding that name. *I think that she was the young lady with a small child,* he mused. Focusing on that name he decided that he would visit that family. Another family in the B category was the name Brode. Yes, he could visit all three families today. With that settled he went about his pursuit.

Time, an element very important to certain industrious minds, had the edge on many; always sneaking up and surprising its captives. Amanda had found herself being one of the captured. Getting out of bed one morning she grasped the reality that soon she would be losing her eldest daughter to college. It was time to do some school shopping. Phoning her sister, Dorthea, a week after the lake incident, she inquired about the two of them making a trip to Hutchinson. Dorthea didn't have to think twice, she too, inclined toward a trip there. Amanda didn't drive which prompted Dorthea to say, "We'll take the Model T."

"Dorthea, please make sure that the seat is fastened down and that the steering wheel is securely in its place."

Dorthea laughed and said, "I'll send Bill out to check everything before we leave."

This was the day for the planned shopping trip. Tootie had been drafted to take care of the household and also to take care of Dorene. John and Eugene were to go and help Mrs. Oberling in the forenoon. That would keep both of them out of trouble and out of Tooties hair for awhile. However, there never was a problem between John and Tootie. They got along fabulously. So fabulously in fact, that Amanda had even held Tootie, who's given name was Elsie, back from starting school until John was old enough, which was the next year. It was Eugene that was the problem for John. He was just a little tag along, as far as he could reason, anyway.

At 9:00 Dorthea and Amanda were on their way. It would take some time to get there. Conversing along the way kept the two entertained. Dorthea, her happiness bubbling over, revealed that she was finally pregnant again. Amanda said, "I'm happy for you Dorthea. You've wanted to add to your family for quite some time. I'm glad that it's you and not me. A while back I thought that I was. It's sort of the wrong time for us to be adding to our family. We've got one going into college. But then a person takes what God gives and is happy about it." The conversation wrapped around that for awhile.

Finally at Hutchinson, they parked and went to a café for a cup of coffee first, sensing that a cup of coffee would perk them up.

Paul, dressed in a pair of navy blue slacks and white sport shirt, looking very handsome, took to his assignment for the day with great anticipation. He'd had his lunch, had already visited the Boling family, and was looking for the Braun residence. Pulling into their driveway he noticed Mrs. Braun mowing the backyard. Vacating his car, he walked towards her. She jumped when she saw a shadow cross her lawn. Seeing that it was the Reverend, she put aside the lawn mower and greeted him.

"Come in. Please come in."

"I don't mean to inconvenience you," Paul replied. "I'm out getting acquainted with my flock. Maybe another time would be more suitable."

"No, no. This will be fine. I need to go in and see about Susan anyway. I put her down for her nap before I started this chore."

He followed her through the back door and into her kitchen.

"We can visit in the living room," she volunteered.

Offering him her favorite chair, she then asked if he'd like a cup of coffee. He declined.

Alice opened the conversation with, "I imagine that it's quite a chore trying to remember everyone?"

"It would have been a pleasure if God would have given me a photogenic mind. But I am thankful for what he has given me and I'm doing rather well."

He went on with, "I have seen you in church with your little one."

"Yes, church is important to us. My husband is in the Army and I need to go to church to hold him up before the Lord every week."

She went on to tell him that he was stationed in Germany and that she hoped that soon he would be coming home, and also relaying her thankfulness to God that the fighting was over in Germany. They talked a bit about Hitler's demise.

Paul, always intent on saving the hopeless, said, "It is really a shame. He could have been saved had he turned to God."

Ending his visit with Alice, Paul said that he'd be looking forward to meeting Gary, her husband, and that he'd continue praying for those who were in the armed forces.

He left and navigated the Ford to the Brode family.

After his visiting was completed, he went to the drug store to drop off the list of hymns for Tamar.

"Who is going to replace you here after you leave for school?" he asked, after their church business had been taken care of.

"I'm not sure. Mr. Simpson has an idea though, I do believe."

"I was just thinking, Rose Abends doesn't quite know what to do with her life at the moment. Maybe she could apply."

"I never thought of that. She'd work out great. I graduated with her, you know."

"I had an idea that you probably did."

"I'll give her a call and suggest that she come in for an interview."

"That might be a good plan," Paul stated.

Finishing his communication with Tamar, Paul went to the grocery store for household items that he needed.

The Brecht's Market, they were also members of his congregation, was an old country type store. There was a pot bellied stove in the center with a couple of benches near by to afford seating for the customers who wished to linger and chat for awhile. Paul relished the various scents that hung between its walls. He was greeted by the Brecht's as he entered. Small talk came forth. He then gave his order, asking for some Beer Kase, also. Even though it was smelly he loved the stuff.

"You'll have to get yourself some beer to go with the cheese, Reverend," Art Brecht stated.

"That cheese will taste just as good with coffee," he replied.

"You haven't lived until you have tried it with beer."

Paul, not interested in changing his life style, smiled, nodded and said, "See you next time around." He left and drove home.

Due to the war, certain items were in scarcity. Things made with rubber were hard to come by. Amanda was looking for elastic. They had tried every department store and there was none to be had. She had made undies for the girls and for herself, using buttons to hold them up. "Well," she said to Dorthea, "I guess that I'll have to resort to buttons again." They had also checked the lingerie department in every store and Amanda was disappointed with what was available, either the wrong size—way too big, or the quality of elastic was undesirable.

They finished up their shopping and with arms loaded down with packages, they headed for the Model T. Amanda sneezed, took a few steps and stopped, saying, "Oh dear."

"What's wrong?" Dorthea asked.

"I think I just lost the button to my underpants."

Letting that soak in for a split second Dorthea then suggested, "Get between those two buildings. I'll walk behind you."

By the time Amanda got between the two buildings she was dragging

her underwear on the ground. She put down her packages, picked up her unmentionables and stuffed them in one of her sacks. She looked at Dorthea and Dorthea just couldn't help it, she busted out laughing. Amanda was embarrassed.

Finally, Dorthea getting her hilarity out of her system, they started for the car again.

"It should have happened to you," Amanda stated. That only brought on another laughing spell.

"Well, it could have been me. I'll go home and sew my buttons on tighter."

"I hope that no one saw me."

"If anyone did they were probably thinking, 'I'm glad that it wasn't me.' "

They continued their drive home with Dorthea bursting out in laughter every once in awhile. "Anyway," Amanda said, "I sure did provide you with laughing material for our trip home."

Dorthea just laughed some more.

Arriving at the Niedlich's, Dorthea walked in with Amanda to pick up Dorene. That's not all that was on her mind. She couldn't wait to tell Tootie about Amanda's mishap. Tootie's face got red but the incident was too funny to let it drop. She laughed too.

"I can't wait to get home to tell Bill," Dorthea said.

"Please don't tell him, Dorthea. That would embarrass me to no end. You have to promise me."

"Okay, Amanda, I won't tell. I'll tell Ma though, the next time I see her."

Amanda had no qualms about that.

Tamar did call Rose to interview for her position. Rose phoned Mr. Simpson for an interview and was granted one for the next day.

Chapter Six

The first Sunday of the month at St. Peter's, was designated communion Sunday. On Saturday afternoon, prior to communion Sunday, communicants were asked to register at the church office if they proposed to take communion. The intention of this practice was to keep the minister abreast with the members who would be partaking. Also, if a minister was in doubt of the inner feelings of any person, a person that might not be in good standing with the Lord, it would become his obligation to counsel that individual before he could partake of the Lord's supper. Receiving the Body and Blood of Jesus was a very solemn, Holy Ordinance and to be entered into as such. It was meant to be kept sacred. Any member with an instinctive sense to confess a grievance, or a sin, this was the proper time to do so.

Announcing in church the Sunday before, Paul conveyed that he would be in the church office on Saturday from 1:00 until 6:00 to receive communicant registration.

In correlation with his announcement, Paul was in his church office on Saturday for this invitation. His church office was a bit smaller than the one in the parsonage. There was a window behind his desk. As he was waiting for his first communicant, he swivelled around in his chair to look out of the window. The west side of the church was in view and from this vantage point he could also see the parsonage. He noticed Maxine going towards the parsonage with something in her hands. Since there were no members around at the moment, he left the church office and walked toward his home. As he approached the building, Maxine was coming out of the front door.

"I thought that you were probably at the church so I let myself in. I made a casserole for you; thought that it might be late after you were finished with your registrations today."

"Thank you very much, Maxine. That was very thoughtful of you. I'm very grateful."

Maxine said, "I came to register for communion."

They walked to the church together, chatting about the beautiful day. Once inside Reverend Riech had her seated, then submitted her name to the registry.

That accomplished and no one else in sight she started a discourse with Paul.

"I'll be leaving for school this month."

"That's right. You're going to beauty school."

"It's not a very long ordeal. As soon as I'm finished I plan on opening a salon in Spruce Island."

"You're not going to open in Anderville?"

"They already have three in Anderville. There's only one in Spruce Island."

Then Maxine became very forward and asked, "How would you like to go fishing?"

Startled by the request Paul said, "I have been doing some fishing. My main goal is to get all of my visitations completed very soon." Not about to give her another chance to spring an invitation of some sort on him, he said, "Maxine, I really need to check on my sermon for tomorrow, if you don't mind. Maybe we can visit at another time. Thanks again for the casserole."

She did mind and left his office a mite offended.

By 6:00 everyone that intended to take communion had registered. Paul closed up the office and walked home.

Eating the hamburger casserole, the token of Maxine Schmit, a knock at the door reached his senses. Receiving the caller, he glanced at Mr. Weise on the other side of the door.

"Good evening, Reverend. We didn't get here in time to register."

"That's quite all right Mr. Weise. Come in. I can do that in my office here."

Ilsa, Ronald and Florence followed Ernst into the house.

One at a time they went into his office to register. Ronald was going into the 12th grade, Florence would be a sophomore. Another girl, Genevieve, who stayed at home, would be in Paul's confirmation class in the fall.

They left after registering and Paul finished his meal.

On Sunday, Paul, his resonant voice in great shape, astoundingly and soundly held the congregation captive with Jesus' parable on the Great Banquet, taken from the 14th chapter of Luke. He felt that this topic fit in well with a communion Sunday. His voice would soften, then rise decibel by decibel. Magnificently unfolding the story, he cast the seed of Jesus' ministry into the hearts of his congeners. The story unfolds as Jesus is conversing with a guest at the Great Banquet. Jesus is telling him that a particular person gave a great dinner and invited many. All those that had been invited had various excuses not to attend. This particular person giving the dinner, became very upset. He told his slave to go out immediately into the streets and invite the poor, the crippled, the blind and the lame. Paul related to the congregation that Jesus was revealing to the banquet party that the souls of man are very precious to Him. Those that are miserably poor and rejected by society shall be as welcomed at His feast as the rich and great.

Ending his sermon eloquently, a hymn was sung and then the Rite of Holy Sacrament had precedence. Tamar played "The Sanctus and the Agnus Dei," the congregation entering in, singing their parts at the appropriate times.

All went well with Reverend Riech serving the Communion Hosts. Nearly to the end Paul had to refill the chalice. Realizing that he had filled it too full, with adept hands he carried it to the first person at the communion rail. He had gripped the cup steadily and by the grace of God, didn't spill a drop. He sent his thanks heavenward.

After the service concluded, Paul again shaking the hands of his flock, Alice Braun, with little Susan, greeted him. Bending over to talk to Susan, she looked at him and said, "You're a ghost,"

"Why Susan," her mother kindly inserted.

"Tell me why you think that I'm a ghost?"

"You gots long dresses on and you talk to a ghost all the time."

"You are definitely paying attention Susan. But I'm not really a ghost." He went on to explain to her that he only wore the robe when he was talking to God's people.

Alice and Paul both shared a laugh. They spoke a few more words, then Paul went on shaking hands with the rest of the congregation.

The Schmit family came up in line, all except Maxine. Gloria again invited him to dinner. This time he could be honest about declining. The Abends family had invited him and he was eagerly looking forward to this invitation.

Soon the church emptied and Tamar, carrying her music, came up to Paul.

"Reverend Riech that was a beautiful sermon. It makes one really think about who comes first."

"It surely does, Tamar. How many Sundays will your presence still be with us?"

Paul noticed that Maxine was standing within hearing range as he asked the question of Tamar.

"Probably for the next two. Mom is planning on a going away dinner. You are invited. I think it's to be a week from this coming Saturday."

"I will definitely save time for that."

They spoke their adios and Maxine stepped up to Paul. Greeting one another, Maxine then revealed to him her frustration about not comprehending the meaning of his sermon.

"Do you think you'd have time to explain it to me?"

"I'm sorry, Maxine. I thought that I had it well clarified. If you stop by the church office on Tuesday morning I'll go over it with you step by step."

"Thank you, Reverend. I had hopes that you could do that today."

"I'm sorry but I have an invitation today."

"Okay, I'll see you Tuesday morning," she said with an edge of disappointment.

The Abends household was cheery as Paul entered. The aroma

coming from the kitchen was titillating. Martin invited him into the living room, offering a comfortable chair.

"You must spend a lot of time on your sermons. They have been great messages."

"I owe all things to God. He inspires me."

They went on talking about Martin's work. He suggested to Paul the confirmation pupils that he felt would be quick learners in his fall class.

Paul, well relaxed, felt that he had a great comrade in Martin. He was aware that he needed a source to impart himself to. Martin seemed the obvious strength.

During the meal, Rose related that she did get the job at the drug store. She thanked Paul for suggesting her. Rose, a bubbly individual, was excited about the new responsibility that she was about to enter.

"I think that you will do very well, Rose," Paul offered.

After a few seconds Martin said, "I hear that you like to fish."

"Yes, I do. I have only been able to go once."

"If you have some time this week maybe we could go. There's a lovely lake not too far from here that I like to visit from time to time."

That was right down Paul's alley. He loved to fish. The two of them made plans for fishing the next day.

Paul's sermon was the topic at the Niedlich dinner table.

Tamar offered, "I read in Isaiah last night: 'He made me a polished arrow.' I thought of Reverend Riech immediately. He sends us polished arrows every Sunday."

"I think that you've got something there Tamar," Herb answered.

Amanda as well acknowledged Tamar's findings, then talked about the going away dinner for her. They settled on a week from Saturday.

"When you go to practice Tamar, you can tell Reverend Riech that we have chosen a day and time for the party."

Tamar and her parents decided that Tamar would play only one more Sunday for the church service, and then give Tootie the joy of getting into the spirit of it.

Monday morning came about clear and sunny. Paul did his usual

morning supplications and then was waiting and ready for Martin.

Once Paul was situated in Martin's automobile, they struck up a conversation about the town of Anderville. Paul having a keen sense about him, filed the information in his mental housing. Since he now was a member of this town he was eager to learn about its development.

Driving toward the lake site, Paul could see why Martin liked this place. It was indeed a heavenly spot.

Both men set about getting their poles and lines in operation. With intentions not to frighten the fish away, they were both very quiet fishermen. Paul's thoughts again turned toward his vocation. Another thought consistently kept cropping up; the thought that Ernst Weise had left with him. What was the rumor that had beset Reverend Weise? Paul sensed that he had a confidential companion in Martin. Maybe asking him about it wouldn't be too unethical.

Fishing over with, Martin and Paul, each with a string of fish, took their leave. Driving down the road, pleased with their day, conversation again was their priority.

Finally, out of curiosity Paul ventured, "Ernst Weise came to visit me awhile back and made some comment about a rumor toward his uncle who had his ministry at St. Peter's."

"Yes, there was a rumor going around. More than likely that's all that it was. We, the people of St. Peter's, that is, are prone to hold men of the cloth on a pedestal. Whatever transpired, was quickly hushed. The party that started the rumor didn't see him in any unlawful act, so to speak. He remained our pastor for awhile but because of it, left his post here a year later.

"I'm glad that I asked about it. It will tend to keep me alert."

"That's a good idea, Reverend."

"Let's do away with formalities, please call me Paul."

"Thanks Paul, I'll certainly befriend you in any issues that create problems for you…in any that I might have knowledge of."

"Thank you, Martin. I'll pray that disturbances of this nature will be easily resolved without leaving any blemishes on my character."

"That will be your best tool."

They continued conversing and soon Martin dropped Paul off at the

parsonage.

"We'll do this again before winter sets in," Martin promised. He then added, "If there is ever anything that you need help with, I'll be more than glad to help."

Paul thanked him.

Settling the state of affairs about Reverend Weise, Paul suddenly realized that his ministry at St. Peter's would be like living in a glass house. Martin was right, prayer would be his best tool. Regardless of where he was, St. Peter's or elsewhere, he knew from the outset that he had chosen a profession where one's integrity needed to be squeaky clean.

Not looking forward to the meeting with Maxine on Tuesday morning, Paul was waiting for her. Once she was off to school in Mankato, he'd feel more relaxed.

Maxine entered the church and Paul met her in the hall. Bible in hand, he ushered her to the church proper and to a pew. He sat down across the aisle from her.

"This is all very simple, Maxine," he began. Starting with the 7th verse, of the 14th chapter in Luke, he read to her from the Bible. "Now then, let me first explain that in the first century banquets often symbolized the kingdom of God. Jesus is really telling His audience not to assume the best seat when you are invited to a dinner. If someone more distinguished comes along and the host would have to move you, what would happen? You'd be embarrassed. At least I would. It would be better to take a less significant seat. The story goes on. Jesus now talks to the host of this banquet, revealing for all to hear, one should invite the poor, the crippled, the lame and the blind. God is concerned for the unfortunate and will exalt anyone who cares for these rather than the more powerful people. I'm sorry that I didn't explain that so that you could understand it. Can you tell me which part puzzles you?"

Maxine, in her subtle way said, "Well I guess I just wasn't paying much attention on Sunday. Now that you have read it to me, I do understand it."

"Good. I'm pleased that you have grasped the meaning."

"Now that we have that taken care of, I thought that I could make lunch for you."

"Maxine, I appreciate your offer but I'm very capable of making my own. I do have some visitations that I need to make this morning."

Feeling that she had been insulted again, face drawn in a frown, she left the church.

Paul was perplexed. What should he do about Maxine? What was her motive?

Tuesday afternoon Dorthea was surprised to see an out-of-state car pull into their driveway. *Wonder who that can be,* she questioned. Watching the man heft himself from the car, she thought, *why that looks like brother Albert.* Stepping outdoors she discovered that it was indeed her brother Albert, his wife Dolores and their infant daughter Shirley, from Seattle, Washington. Excitement ensued.

Quickly hugging her brother, she said, "What are you doing here?"

"We're on our way to settle down in North Dakota near Dolores' parents. Just wanted to stop to see everyone here first."

"Well, come on in," she excitedly exclaimed.

Albert introduced his wife to his sister. The couple had been married in Seattle where they had met.

That evening there was a gathering of relatives at Bill and Dorthea's, everyone wanting a chance to meet Dolores and to visit with Albert.

Wednesday afternoon Reverend Riech had again taken the hymn numbers to Tamar at the drug store, visiting for awhile as usual. She relayed to him that her Uncle, Aunt and their baby girl had driven all the way from Seattle, Washington, and that they were leaving the next day. Especially fond of her uncle, she was sorry that Reverend Riech wouldn't get a chance to meet them.

After Albert and Dolores left the next morning, Tamar took the family car and drove to church to practice. The Reverend was in his study. Stepping into his office, smiling, she greeted him and handed him an apple pie that she had baked.

"Good morning, Tamar. It's good to see you. Thank you kindly for the apple pie."

"You're very welcome. I've come to practice. Mom wanted me to tell you that the going away dinner will be a week from Saturday."

"Great! I'll be there."

"Are your Aunt and Uncle still visiting?"

"No, they left for North Dakota this morning. They are going to stay with her parents until my Uncle gets established in a new job."

"That shouldn't be hard to do with a shortage of men."

Tamar went on to tell him that her Uncle had a dysfunctional arm. His left arm, that hung rather limply, was the reason why Uncle Sam didn't want him fighting this war. It had been injured as a youngster.

The conversation ended, Tamar went to practice, Paul continued writing his sermon.

A car pulled into the church yard. From his office window Paul could see that it was Maxine again. He stayed seated in his office.

Maxine, with a purposeful walk, went over to Tamar at the organ.

"I saw your car here and thought that I would stop. I was on my way into town to get some canning supplies for Mother," she announced.

Tamar stopped playing and greeted her, then said, "I need to get my practicing in before I go to work. When are you going to school?"

"I'm leaving in about a week. I'll be home most weekends though. Mankato isn't all that far away."

"Well, maybe we'll get to see each other once in awhile. I'm coming home some weekends too."

"Have you been able to talk to Reverend Riech much?"

"A little. Why?"

"I just think that he's very rude."

"Why do you say that?"

"I wanted him to explain his sermon to me and he wasted no time in chasing me away."

"I can't imagine Reverend Riech being like that."

"Well, I just wanted to see if he's like that with everybody."

"Give him some time, Maxine. I'm sure that he struggles trying to make the acquaintance of all of the members."

"I'll see if I give him more time. He's been very rude to me."

"Maxine, please don't make things more difficult for him. I really feel

that he's trying very hard."

Tamar tried her best to reason with Maxine.

Finally, taking Tamar's words to heart, for the moment anyway, they both left the church.

Paul noting that both girls were leaving the church, continued on with his desk obligations.

Still perplexed about Maxine he held her up to the Lord in prayer after he finished his studies.

Chapter Seven

This was the day that all America had been waiting for. On this day, the 14th of August, 1945, Japan had surrendered. News of the surrender arriving on the streets of Anderville around 6:00 p.m., pandemonium prevailed. Horns were honking, bells were ringing, people were shouting. Boys with bicycles, tin cans tied behind them, were riding up and down the streets, making their noise as well. John and Bobby were amongst them with Eugene tagging on their tail. Citizens forgoing their supper and meal preparations, stepped out of their homes, grabbed their neighbors, hugging them. A few farmers left their posts, going into town to be part of the clamor. The war was over. America was still a free country. Women waiting for their husbands to come home, mothers for their sons and daughters, would soon see that reality. They would come home and take up their rightful place in the community.

Amongst all of the cheering a loud bang brought Amanda to attention.

"What was that?" she asked of Tootie.

"It sounds like it came from Ruals place."

Ruals lived next door to the Niedlich's. Their house was made of stone and was one of the older homes in Anderville.

Amanda and Tootie started walking toward the Ruals. Noticing Mrs. Ruals running out of the house, they hastened their walk.

"What happened?" Amanda asked her.

"With all of the commotion I guess I forgot to light the burner to the stove. Gus came in with his cigarette burning and the gas ignited."

"Is Gus okay?"

Just then Gus came out and explained that it knocked him back. His

hand was a bit numb but he thought that he was okay.

Amanda said, "Well, you certainly can be thankful!"

Part of the kitchen wall was damaged, other than that all seemed to be satisfactory.

"I know," Amanda said, "you were wanting to put everyone else to shame. You gave this day the loudest bang."

Everyone laughed.

Soon more neighbors joined them.

Word got around town that there would be a church service at St. Peter's the following evening. A service to renew one's faith and to send praises to God who had again shown the American people that the motto, In God We Trust, was a stronghold.

Reverend Riech phoned Tamar and gave her the hymns that were to be sung that evening. Tamar quickly went over the hymns on the old pump organ. Paul had chosen, "A Mighty Fortress Is Our God," and "Glorious Things Of Thee Are Spoken, Zion City Of Our God." Although God Bless America was not in the Lutheran Hymnal, they would sing it. Paul felt assured that everyone knew the song by heart.

Most of the residents of Anderville entered the next day with happy hearts. The war was definitely over. Paul had put together a great service for the "Blessing of Peace" service. The church was filled.

Shortly after the big peace celebration on the streets of Anderville, Maxine left for Mankato where she would be learning cosmetology. Paul did give her a big send off, telling her that he wished her well in her new endeavor.

Several days after the V-J Day doings, Paul was looking for material to read. He liked reading about historical events and people. *I'll visit the library and see what they have to offer,* was his thought.

Walking into the library he noticed a young woman, whom he guessed to be about twenty-five, or there about, at the desk. He spoke to her. Paul asserted that he was looking for books on the Blackfoot Indians, any of the Indian uprisings and maybe something on Abraham Lincoln.

She was able to help him and he chose four books.

"My, you do a lot of reading don't you?"

Smiling at her he said, "The mind is a fine instrument. To keep it stimulated one must feed it from time to time."

"That is true." Then realizing that he must be the new minister in town, she said, "You must be Reverend Riech?"

"I am. And you are?"

"I'm Vivian Lute. I'm very pleased to make your acquaintance."

They went on visiting for a small portion of an hour. Paul then picked up his books and left.

Vivian was a widow. Her husband, Jim, had been in the war operation in the Philippines and was killed soon after he arrived in that country. A very attractive red-head, she was attired in a green suit and white blouse. Slim and trim like Paul, she stood at 5' 6" inches. Her smile was captivating.

Paul left and thought about this young lady, how sad it was for her to lose a mate, thinking too, how sensible and kind she seemed to be.

Going to the grocery store, he picked up the few items that he needed, then he hurried on home.

The garden still producing eatables, Amanda had picked the string beans that had come on later. She and Tamar were sitting outdoors snapping them, their conversation turning to Tamar leaving home soon. Like her own mother's discussion to her on private matters, Amanda was passing on the information to Tamar. It wasn't often that they were alone to talk of such matters. Realizing that Tamar was a responsible adult, Amanda felt that the subject still needed to be broached. They talked freely, no one disturbing them. Of course, most of this conversation wasn't new to Tamar. Her Aunt Dorthea was a good source of information. Tamar had spent a lot of time with her before and after Dorene was born.

On Sunday, Tootie amazed everyone with her knack at the board-of-ivories. She was definitely controlling the organ and appeared very confident. Paul thanked her.

Knowing that his encouragement wasn't a necessity, he did so anyway, telling her she did a splendid job. Tamar was certain that she had lost her job but was very thankful that her sister had done so well.

All too quickly the going away party for Tamar arrived. She was excited and filled with awe on that night. Amanda had prepared a great dinner. Carl and Sophia Platz, Bill, Dorthea and Dorene, Reverend Riech, were there. Amanda's brother, Fred, and his wife, Freida, who lived on a farm thirteen miles away, had also been invited and were there as well.

An enjoyable meal, followed by a "singspiration" made the evening a time to remember. Tamar recorded the evening in her journal. Reverend Riech had offered a heartfelt prayer for her. She had tears in her eyes and thanked him graciously. Patting her on the shoulder, he said, "Tamar, I'll miss your kindred spirit. I'm sure your family will miss you as well. You have a very giving heart and will do well. I'll pray for that."

Things in general went back to some sort of semblance after Maxine and Tamar left for other parts of Minnesota. Missing Tamar more than she realized, Amanda would phone Dorthea more often than usual. Tootie, John and Eugene were back in school, with Ruth home for yet another year. Spending more time with Ruth, Amanda schooled her in numbers and the alphabet. Quite often the two of them would walk to Carl and Sophia's to visit with them.

Dorthea's pregnancy was coming along, but to a considerable extent she felt pregnant. She lagged behind in her work and often would go into town to pick up Amanda and Ruth to help her out. Milking cows, feeding chickens, gathering eggs and the everlasting job of cleaning eggs, chores that were forever staring her in the face. The milk separator and milk pails needed washing. Since there was no porch to enter before going into the kitchen from the outdoors, mopping the kitchen floor was almost a daily necessity. Getting Amanda to help from time to time, was an advantage for Dorthea.

Driving out to the farm one day Dorthea said, "Amanda, I'm going to teach you how to drive. That would be a good thing—being able to

drive."

"Well, whenever you're ready."

"I have too much going on today or I'd take the time right now. Maybe you should ask Herb first...see if we can use your car."

"I'm sure that he wouldn't mind. I'll ask him though."

Ruth and Amanda spent happy days with Dorthea. She was always laughing about something.

One day while washing the woodwork, Amanda said, "I'll wash the banister."

Dorthea, with her head stuck between bedding, didn't hear her properly and thought she said that she would wash the minister. That brought on a fit of laughter.

"Dorthea, I swear, that baby is going to come out laughing." So went their time together.

At home that evening, at the supper table, Amanda said, "Dorthea wants to teach me how to drive."

"It might be a good idea. With the war over with, gas should be more plentiful soon."

"She wants to teach me with our car."

"I'd say that is the best idea."

That was settled.

Paul's confirmation class was held on Thursday afternoons, right after school let out. His new class consisted of Tootie, John, Genevieve Weise, Warren Abends, Phillip Schmit, John's pal, Bobby Otts and Lewis Erst. There were no second year conferments for the fall.

Lewis Erst was the son of Tom and Luella Erst. Paul was acquainted with this family and had made a visitation at their home. Tom worked wherever he could find a job, working at the lumber company part time. Luella did housecleaning for several people in town, her clients being Dr. Myers, and the dentist, Dr. Jeffrey. Paul had been informed that Tom was a drinker and to be prepared of the problem when he went to pay them a visit. He didn't need to be advised of the poser, he immediately detected the offense. Lewis was their only child.

On Friday morning Dorthea came into town with the idea that she was going to teach Amanda how to drive. Her concept was to let Amanda do for herself from the start.

"Okay, Amanda. I'll show you how to operate this car."

"Shouldn't you back it out of the garage for me first?"

"You can do that."

They both got in the car, Dorthea showing her how to clutch and brake, and how to change gears.

That part of the lesson over with she introduced her to the steering wheel and starter.

"Now you're ready. Start it up and back out. At least you don't have to crank this car."

"Dorthea, won't you please back it out for me?"

"All right."

They switched places, Dorthea backing it out like an ole' pro. She shut off the motor, wanting Amanda to do it from the top.

Trading places again with Amanda behind the wheel, she started the car. Dorthea instructed her in maneuvering the car.

"You're doing fine, Amanda."

Amanda was doing great, that is until she went to turn a corner, running over the curb and on the edge of their neighbors lawn. Dorthea laughed and said, "Be careful. I'm in no condition to push you out of a bad situation."

Steering the car evenly on the road, Amanda managed to get the car to the creamery. The creamery provided a lot of space to move the car about. Working it to and fro she did better and Dorthea said, "Now you can drive out to the farm."

Amanda had walked Ruth over to her parents home earlier, and Dorthea had dropped Dorene off there on her way into town. The two ladies had the day to themselves. Dorthea needed help on the farm again. Amanda was a great seamstress and busied herself making a smock for her sister.

At home that evening, Herb asked Amanda how her driving lesson went. Amanda confessed of her mishap, saying also, that she did well driving out to the farm and back home. Herb breathed a sigh of relief.

Chapter Eight

Reaping the fruits of their labor, Bill and Dorthea had their corn cribs filled, hay was in the loft, oats and barley were in the granary. But not without the help of the Niedlich family. In need of help from time to time, Herb getting off from his day's work, the children out of school for the day, they would all go out to the country to help out.

Fall harvesting placed good feelings in Tamar's heart. A bit melancholy, when home from school one weekend, she realized that this year's harvesting had gone by without her help. Fashioning teepees, as she called them, from the bundles of oats, along with her father, Uncle Bill, John and Tootie, was a time for counting blessings. It was a time to thank God that He had again provided for her aunt and uncle and for her family as well.

On these occasions Amanda and Dorthea saw to setting food on the table. Dorthea was a good cook and the Niedlichs enjoyed eating from her table.

The Beck's home was an old country styled house with a bedroom downstairs along with a dining room/living room combination, a kitchen and pantry. Two bedrooms upstairs and an attic, completed their country home.

Dorthea, knowing that Tamar loved her carrot/raisin cake recipe, always made sure there was a raisin/carrot cake at harvest time. Smoked sausages from their smoke house was also a great treat.

Other cornfields still dotted the surrounding landscape with their need of picking. Halloween and Winter were nearing. In fact, snow had already appeared.

Tamar had been home for a couple of weekends and had assumed her position as organist on those Sundays. School was going well for her.

True to her word, Maxine was home almost every weekend. She had again proposed an outing with Paul and he had refused her yet again. Feelings torn into shreds, she concentrated on what she might do to throw his heart into a dither.

Visiting the library several times, Paul was becoming quite familiar with Vivian Lute. She was a most gracious person and they conversed rather well on several subjects.

Paul had the faculty about him to watch his comings and goings. Given what had been revealed to him about Reverend Weise, he had best watch his step; although he didn't have any idea what the incident was about. Praying constantly, he prayed that his ways would be God's ways and that no ill rumors would be obtained from his actions. Because they conversed so well, Paul, hungry for conversation that would lift him to higher mental plateaus, appreciated Vivian's verbal, electrified input. It was in his mind to ask her out to dinner, hoping that they could have uninterrupted time to chat. Thus far no one knew of their friendship, Paul usually visiting the library when there was no one else around.

Going to the library early one morning, he picked out a couple of books, ultimately chatting with Vivian. No one else being around, making it an opportune time to request her presence at supper that evening. She accepted.

Knowing full well that this could trigger gossip, he planned on taking her to Hutchinson and away from gawking eyes, he hoped. Their relationship was purely platonic, a mental issue, no amorous love involved. Paul had prayed about this conversational thing that they had going. He had the inner peace that God would not be angry with his move.

At 6:00 that evening he drove to pick her up. The streets were dark and he hoped that no one would uncover this happening. The less people knew of his involvement the better.

Traveling to Hutchinson they conversed on a number of subjects. Paul, finding a café that seemed rather quiet, parked his Ford, opened the door for Vivian and gave her a hand getting out of the car.

Entering the café, Paul found a quiet table in the back that looked suitable. Helping Vivian off with her fur coat, exposing a beautiful green/navy plaid skirt and navy cardigan. He held her chair for her. She looked strikingly beautiful and her smile was dazzling. The waitress, taking their order, thought them a nice looking couple.

Conversation took over.

"If you don't mind my asking, you said that you were born in Iowa City, how did you happen to relocate to Anderville?" Paul asked of her.

"I met Jim when he was in college. We fell in love and married and moved to Anderville. It was his hometown. He was drafted shortly after we moved. I liked Anderville and just stayed on," she responded giving away her captivating smile.

She had attended a church service once and was taken by Paul's moving sermon.

They conversed about that for awhile, Vivian giving her thoughts on some of his deliberations.

"I'm curious and have to ask, which church in our fair town do you belong to?"

"I'm the direct opposite of yours. I am a member of St. Mary's. I hope that doesn't make a difference?"

"I'm pretty broad minded about religions. There are things that I will sway away from in our conversations though."

"I'm pretty level headed about our differences too. But the Catholic church really does hold her own."

"I'm well aware of that fact."

They talked on about Martin Luther and his connection with the Catholic church, going on with some reading that Paul had been enlightened with, like Thomas Jefferson and Andrew Jackson.

"I'm always amazed at the men who led our country with little or no higher education, like Andrew Jackson. His education was sporadic. Abraham Lincoln, also, was more or less self taught," Paul stated.

"Then there is Thomas Jefferson who studied at the college of William and Mary. He was not a polished orator, preferring to use the pen instead of making speeches," Vivian offered.

"See the contrast, Abe with his home schooling, making some very

impressive speeches," Paul inserted.

And so it went. The night wore on and it was time to head back to Anderville.

Once home that evening, Paul thought about the encounter with Vivian. She had this smile that would knock any man off of his feet. *If things were only different*, he thought. *To the majority, Catholicism and Lutheranism just don't mix. Maybe years from now things will be different.* The evening did provide food for thought. He did need some outside interests. He felt that, if differently, he would become a boring old man. And too, he knew how the town would react toward a Lutheran and a Catholic together. He had seen glimpses of it in this town already. But certainly, she had already stolen a piece of his heart. Leaving his thoughts behind he prepared for bed.

Halloween arrived. Having a plan in her head, Maxine made her way clear to be home for that day. Gathering her brother into her secretive plans, he was not as gamely as she was for this notion. But he, along with Maxine, proceeded with her scheme.

John and Bobby had their plans also. Hearing a rumor that Reverend Riech was going to be the target by some no-good trespassers, Bobby and John planned on throwing the culprits into orbit by scaring the daylights out of them. However, no one knew who the predators were.

Near the church there was a graveyard. One could clearly see the parsonage from that vantage point.

A full moon brightened the night. Bobby and John, dressed warmly, white sheets thrown over them, took their flashlights and walked toward the graveyard. A car coming from the opposite direction made them jump in the ditch. After all, they weren't the rascals and were only defending their minister. No need getting caught. Arriving at the cemetery they waited behind a rather large tombstone. The parsonage was dark, they assumed that Reverend Riech was gone. Perhaps the car that had approached them was Reverend Riech, they reasoned.

Faint lights coming from the other side, were noticeable to them. They watched.

The moving figures came closer. Still they were unable to see who it

was. The unknown forms moved about in back of Paul's house, getting ready to do their misdeed.

"Come on let's go," John voiced.

White sheets flapping in the air, screaming like banshees, John and Bobby advanced towards the parsonage. All misery broke loose. Maxine and her brother Phillip, frightened to the extent of heart failure, ran like crazy. In doing so Maxine didn't see the clothesline, ran right into it, catapulting her backwards with her bucket of horse manure, emptying itself on her and the snowed ground. She screamed, using some unmentionable words as well. Phillip ran to help her up. Grabbing the bucket, faster than lightening they ran for home. John and Bobby laughed until their sides ached. They still couldn't see who the offenders were.

The next morning, looking out of the kitchen window, Paul noticed that he had been paid a visit. Putting on his old coat, he got a shovel and cleaned up the offensive looking sight, disposing of it in the garden area. Come spring he would dig it into the soil. Of course he wondered who might dislike him enough to come up with a deed that nasty. He'd let it drop. No harm done.

Although the two boys, too, would like to have known the names of the persons involved in this conspiracy, they never mention the incident to anyone.

Rose's bubbly personality worked out to her advantage at the drug store. She loved what she was doing. College now was not in the making for her. She had just received a letter from her beau with the news that he was coming home. No one knew of her involvement with Joe Caridin. He was Catholic, she was Lutheran. Rose knew that the reality of her involvement with Joe would be very disappointing to her parents. She loved her folks and didn't want to distress them. But being so in love with Joe she wasn't about to give him up. His letters, filled with love for her, were never sent directly to the Abends home. Joe's sister, Mary, received them and delivered them to Rose. Before he had been drafted, the two were only seen with other people, roller skating, ice skating, visiting the hamburger shop for soda's and such. They would occasionally slip away to be alone to talk about life together for them, both of them knowing

what a problem this would create. And now he was coming home. What should she do? Maybe she could talk to Reverend Riech. After all, her father and Reverend were good friends. Well, she'd think about this for awhile.

Chapter Nine

Along with fall came the start-up of Sunday School. Martin Abends took over the position of superintendent. He had his recruits, the Sunday School teachers, taking their positions on Sunday mornings. There were six classes. Paul and Martin often discussed how things were progressing. Reasoning that he had an excellent counter-part in Martin, Paul occasionally sought his expertise. They were becoming very good friends.

The choir was off to a great start, Paul taking over the leadership since not a single one of the members had that musical ability. They were already rehearsing Christmas pieces. The Niedlichs, Becks, Martin and Laura Abends, Maxine's mom, Gloria, Ilsa and Ronald Weise, and Alice Braun, made up the body of singers. Alice brought little Susan with her. She was a well behaved child, looking at books while they practiced. Of course the adults took time to talk with her too, especially Paul. He often would say, "Come Susan and help me direct this choir." She was willing. It gave a good break in between songs, with the adults eagerly encouraging her.

Following choir practice one evening, Laura not being able to keep her commitment that evening, Martin lingered afterwards. He and Paul liked discussing world issues as well as church functions. On this particular night the two men talked about music. Together they harmonized very well on several German songs they had picked out. "O du frohliche" was a favorite. They talked about singing it in German for the Christmas Day service, but since the war with Germany was still so fresh in the minds of people, Paul felt that it wasn't the best of ideas. When the war started with Germany, many of the churches that were still providing German services

for their members, had to discontinue them. There were people of other nationalities who noticeably avoided people who were of German descent, even tormenting them with underhanded acts, such as painting the swastika on their front doors. Paul brought up that fact and then said, "Maybe the two of us can do a duet for the Christmas Day Service. We could sing, 'Lobt Gott, ihr Christen' and sing it in English, 'Praise God the Lord Ye Sons of Men.'"

"Sounds like a good one to me," Martin answered him. So it was planned.

With the summer months over with, Paul had taken down the porch swing, storing it in the basement along with the wicker chairs.

Church functions kept him busier and he hadn't had time to visit the library. He knew that one day soon he would have a need to seek its internal written work for mind improvement. He was already aware that he'd have to spend less time with Vivian. She deserved a good man of her own assemblage, he couldn't be tying up her time. That would be unfair to her. He'd make it a point to talk to her.

One day as he was in town picking up groceries, he saw Tom Erst stumbling out of a tavern. As he wobbled all over the place, Paul decided to give him a lift home. Whatever people thought, so be it. Jesus' association with the tax collector, Zacchaeus, made Paul aware of the fact that Jesus never walked away from the underprivileged or the sinners. He would play the good Samaritan for his neighbor. At least Jesus would say that Tom was his neighbor regardless of the four and a half mile distance between them. Tom was reluctant to get in the car, but ultimately swayed his way into the front seat.

"I see the fallacious spirit has got a tight grip on you, Tom," Paul asserted.

"I'm do-un fi-nn," he stammered.

"Perhaps you need to get rid of that tiger that's got you by the tail."

"Mi-ight be-e."

No more was said. Paul saw him to the door. Shaking his head as he left, he thought about Luella. What a fine person she was. Their son Lewis

was doing well in his confirmation class. He knew that it had to be hard on him too.

Luella, fully aware of Tom's problem, would confiscate his whiskey bottles and hide them. She had numerous bottles hidden about the house. Tom never asked about them, but then, he never wanted her to know that he drank. What a hypothetical idea that was, everyone knew that he drank.

The Thursday afternoon confirmation class was going well. Their study on repentance and forgiveness raised a lot of questions. Phillip was conscience stricken. His mind was playing tricks on him. *Why did I ever let Maxine talk me into dumping that manure on Reverend's lawn?* he asked himself. It was on his mind night and day. *I have to tell someone. But I gave my word to Maxine. What should I do?*

He was so disturbed that finally he made his confession to Reverend Riech. Paul was astounded since he felt that Phillip had his senses about him. "I forgive you Phillip," Paul relayed to him. "I believe your sister owes me an apology as well."

"I don't want her to know that I told you."

"Seeing that it was a Halloween night and all sort of things going flying in the night then, I'll not betray you, Phillip."

Phillip had told him about the two ghosts that scared them to death, yet had no idea who they were. He withheld the fact that if the ghosts had not appeared, his back steps would have received the deposit of horse manure, Maxine hoping that he would accidentally step in it.

During a break in their studies, Phillip revealed his secret to the boys in the class. John and Bobby were surprised at his confession, but were enlightened that the mystery now had been solved. They didn't reveal that they had been the ghosts in question.

Conversation about Reverend's Halloween ordeal, was the table talk at the Niedlich's supper table that evening.

"Why would she want to do such a thing?" Amanda asked.

"I don't know. But Phillip said that she thought Reverend Riech was very rude."

"Where did she get such an idea?" Herb asked.

John had no answer. Amanda remarked that confessions and forgiveness makes one's heart clean, that this was a good lesson for their family too. "We all make mistakes now and then," she voiced.

November entered the Niedlich establishment with a flurry of excitement as well as activities. Robert was coming home on furlough. Amanda's brother Rufus was returning home to resume his life as it had been before wartime. Just out of high school, he wasn't sure where this life would take him. Dorthea and Sophia were equally in a dither, getting things ready for his return. Since Robert was going to be home about the same time, Amanda said that she would have the "Welcome Home Party" for Rufus. They would celebrate both gatherings together.

Sophia was an archaic housekeeper, going over her duties quickly, her home was always in order. She also managed a small garden in the summer-time as well; a space that they rented from one of the church members. She had made pickles, canned tomatoes and beans during the summer. Everyone loved Sophia's pickles.

Alma Rille, was a very good friend of Sophia's and had been so for many years. She, like Sophia, had lots of children. Alma's were all boys but one. A couple of the Rille boys were friends of Rufus and they too, were coming home from the war front. Sophia and Alma had a lot to talk about. Herman, Alma's husband, ran the meat shop in Anderville, along with Alma's help. Sophia would rescue her on occasions, Alma having her hands full with the younger boys still at home. The Rilles' were also members of St. Peter's. The church needing to be cleaned before Easter each year, the two ladies often went to give their support.

Sophia's children were all married except Rufus and the youngest daughter, Margret—they called her Margie. The Platz family was spread around the United States, one daughter in South Dakota, one in Northern Minnesota, two daughters in Indiana, a son, Albert, who had just moved to North Dakota and two sons that farmed outside of Anderville.

The Saturday before Thanksgiving the big homecoming party took over Amanda's household. A big dinner was planned for that evening, rabbit being the main course. Dorthea was bringing the salads. Sophia

would bring part of the dessert and also her sweet and dill pickles. Amanda's two brothers, Fred and Walter, and their families, who farmed outside of Anderville, would bring dessert also. Clara, Amanda's sister, the third in birth, and her husband, Edwin, and children, would bring rolls. Reverend Riech had also been invited. Margie, Amanda's youngest sister, came from Fort Wayne for Thanksgiving and for the party as well. She and Rufus were great pals.

Robert and Rufus had already arrived home several days before. The two sought each others company, Robert taking in all that Rufus offered about Germany, knowing that he'd be leaving Texas for foreign soil as soon as his furlough was over.

Tamar came home that weekend, helping Amanda wherever help was needed. Everyone was in a party mood and enjoying the company as well as the good food. Rufus, Robert and the Reverend spent time getting acquainted.

Paul soon found Tamar sitting on the sofa. He sat down in a vacant chair beside her and asked, "How is school going?"

"I'm really enjoying it."

They talked on about some of the biblical questions in one of her classes, discussing some of the prophets and the lives of St. Paul, John and Peter as well.

"I can tell that you are going to be an exceptional teacher, Tamar," Paul opined.

"I certainly hope that I do a good job. I can see where it's a big undertaking, rooting truthful and ethical principals into the minds of young children. I don't want to fail them."

"If you have that sense about you, Tamar, you'll do just fine."

They talked on about other things, Paul's mother coming for Thanksgiving and the fact that his sister wouldn't be able to get away to join them. He also stated that he would be going to Milwaukee for a few days right after Christmas and hoped that his sister would be able to be with them. Tamar caught sight of the fact that he had great respect for his mother. She had heard the saying, "If you want to find a good husband, find a man who is good to his mother." Paul would surely make someone a good husband, she felt.

It was a great party and everyone was so relieved that Rufus came home in one piece. Talking with his sister, Margie, she encouraged him to move to Fort Wayne, Indiana. She was positive that he could find work there. Rufus was interested.

The Wednesday before Thanksgiving, Paul met his mother at the bus depot. He hugged her tenderly and helped her to the car.

After getting his mother settled in the guest bedroom, he whisked her off to a café for their evening meal. Having much to talk about they seemed never to run out of words.

Following the church service on Thanksgiving Day, Paul and his mother joined the Abends family for dinner. Laura found Mrs. Riech to be an easy person to be around. Visiting freely with her, Laura said, "Your son is a remarkable young man."

"I'm sure it is because I prayed the presence of God into him," she answered.

"Oh, that's what makes him so special!" Laura declared.

The dinner's main course was two ducks with two different types of dressing. Laura's expertise in the culinary art went over great. Having satisfied their appetite, the men thanked Laura for the great meal and retired to the living room where a discourse on the world situation ensued.

Rose and Mrs. Riech helped Laura clear the table. Dishes washed and put away, Rose asked to be excused, saying that she wanted to go and see her friend, Mary. Laura gave her permission.

Rose's heart did flip-flops on her walk over to the Caridins. No one was exactly sure when Joe would be getting home. She hoped that it would be soon. The snow crunched beneath her feet as she hastened her walk.

Mary met her at the door and they hugged each other. Rose removed her overshoes, tweed coat and white stocking cap with diamond shaped designs of maroon and aqua knitted into it.

After greeting Mary's parents the two girls departed for Mary's bedroom. In secret they discussed the latest news on Joe.

"He'll be home any day now," Mary remarked.

"I'm so excited and yet quite fearful. I don't know how to tell my parents. You know, he wants to get married as soon as he returns?"

"I suspected that. He has to tell our parents too. When do you think you'll get married?"

"I'll wait until Joe gets home and we'll decide together."

And so they talked, making small plans for the wedding.

Chapter Ten

Propelled with vim and vigor the Niedlichs bathed their home in a festive Christmas panorama. Although Robert had to return to his base in Texas, Rufus was home for good. The war was over and this Christmas celebration would be marked with great songs of joy. Christ had come to redeem all men, even evil men like Hitler, and the Niedlichs would pour their souls and voices into rapturous praise to God. Life was good!

Maxine was home for the Holidays. Tamar would soon be home as well. Rose was still waiting for her Joe to return. As yet, she hadn't told her parents about the wedding that was soon to come about.

On Friday Paul was in his study preparing for Sunday's service, as well as for the Christmas Eve and Christmas Day services. Maxine, en route to the Brecht's store, took notice of Paul's car in front of the church as she passed by. She stopped, backed up, drove in and parked beside his car.

Paul noticing that she had parked in front of the church, watched as she walked in. His office door was open. He raised a prayer to God that there would be no confrontation with Maxine.

"Hi," she excitedly voiced.

"Hello, Maxine. What brings you here? Thought that you'd have lots of shopping to do?"

"No, I have all my shopping done. I'm on my way to the store for Mom. Just thought I'd stop in and say hello."

"How's school going?"

"It's great! I learned how to cut hair. So if you're in need of a trim I'd

gladly do that for you."

"I'm going home right after the Christmas Day service and will have my hair cut in Milwaukee."

"Oh, so we Andervillions aren't good enough to cut your hair?"

"It's not that, Maxine. I have already had my hair cut in Anderville. I just don't have time to do it now. I'm very busy."

"Oh, sorry. I'll leave you to your speech making."

"I'm happy that school is going great for you. See you at church Sunday."

Maxine left still feeling resentment. *Why won't he give me the time of day?* she wondered.

On Sunday the church was filled. Pastor Riech based his sermon on man's fallen condition and the angel Gabriel's visitation to Mary. Maxine, seated close to the front with her parents, seemed to be absorbed in the preachment. Looking over his congregation Paul caught a glimpse of Vivian, the librarian, seated near the back. For a moment his heart jumped to his throat. Gaining control of his senses directly, he went on with his sermon.

The service ended. Paul, standing at the back of the church, was greeting his flock.

The Schmidt family hastened to greet him. Phillip was one of his more studious students in his confirmation class. He greeted him warmly.

Maxine had remained behind to talk with Tamar who had arrived home on Saturday. Tootie, focused on finishing the postlude, noticed Tamar standing near, waiting for her to finish.

Alice, along with her husband Gary, who was carrying Susan, stepped up to Paul.

"I see your husband made it home safely," he said to Alice as he shook her hand.

To Gary he said, "It's so nice to have you back. I'm sure that your family is thrilled at your arrival home just in time for Christmas."

Gary took his hand, shaking it whole heartily, and said, "It's wonderful to be home, just wonderful! Nice to make your acquaintance, too." They spoke a few more sentences and then left, Alice placing her hand in the

crook of his arm.

Vivian walking up to Paul, extended her hand, saying, "You approached your scripture selections in an amazing fashion."

"Thank you, Vivian. Of course you realize that my help comes from above." He continued with, "It's nice to see you again."

"You must not be doing any reading. I haven't seen you in awhile."

"With Christmas and New Year services to prepare for I really haven't had the time."

"Yes, I can see where it is a busy time for you."

"I'm going home for a few days right after Christmas service on Tuesday. I'll probably be in sometime next week."

"I'll be looking for you."

While they were talking Maxine had her eyes fixated on them. *Is he going with that Catholic?* she wondered. Her thoughts were not good ones.

Paul greeted Tootie, again thanking her. Tamar was next in line. Maxine, wanting to be alone when she greeted Paul, stepped back and waited for the church to empty.

"Nice to see you, Tamar. You are playing for the Christmas Day service?"

With a big smile she enthusiastically said, "Nice to see you again. Yes, I'm playing on Christmas Day."

"Why don't you wait a few minutes and I'll get the hymns for you."

"Okay."

She stepped aside.

Paul walked over to where Maxine was standing and extended his hand.

"Good morning, Maxine."

"Reverend Riech, are you going with that Catholic?"

He was slightly stunned, and after a moment said, "Maxine, she isn't a 'that.' Her name is Vivian." Exasperated with her pettiness, he continued with, "It should be of no concern to you that I befriend her. Jesus himself associated with people who were not of the same mind that he was. If you'll excuse me I have other things to attend to." He walked up to Tamar, placed a hand on her shoulder and said, "Okay Tamar, follow me." She followed him to his office.

Maxine sullenly walked away as her eyes followed Paul and Tamar moving toward his office. She was envious.

Paul and Tamar chatted for awhile and Paul noticed for the first time, the pair of dimples she had when she smiled. He couldn't remove his eyes from her face. Handing her the list of hymns he then said, "It's so nice to have your presence with us again," all the while wondering why he hadn't noticed her dimples before.

"Why thank you, Reverend. It's always nice to be home."

Once home, Paul sat down and thought about the morning service. Maxine tripped through his mind. He really hadn't meant to be so abrupt with her. Sitting behind his desk, leaning back in his chair, hands locked behind his head, he thought, *I don't know how I can ease her mind in a different direction. Dear God, what can I do?* He then thought about Vivian. She made his heart thump. *Surely God, this isn't what you want for me, is it?* Then he thought about Tamar. She was probably all of eight years, or more, younger than he. *Of course men marry women even ten years younger,* he thought. *Joseph was quite a bit older than Mary.* He bowed his head and asked that God would guide him in all of his actions.

He left his prayer in God's hands and went to fix his lunch. *A wife would be a good thing for me. That would get Maxine out of my hair,* was his thinking.

Monday was the 24th. House cleaning day for Paul. He hurried through it. There was much to do this day.

Having finished his cleaning he gave the rest of the day to the evening service. A five foot tall Christmas tree had been put up in the church sanctuary. The altar paraments had been changed to white to go with the Christmas season. Paul checked to make sure that the hymnals were in place. The janitors, John and Anna Lutz, had everything in place. God's house was ready for the program which the children would perform that evening. Excitement filled the air and Paul walked home to ready for the evening.

Paul was already in the church office when the Abends arrived at church an hour before the program was to begin. Martin instructed the entire family on filling sacks with an apple, an orange, peanuts and a small

amount of candy for the Sunday School children.

Rose was energized. She knew that Joe was to be home at any moment. The last word that she received from Joe was that if he couldn't connect with a bus or train he'd hitch hike home. She had high hopes that he would make it for Christmas. Nervous energy assisted her and her mind was never far from Joe.

The Niedlich family, ready for the evening, hurried to the car. Tootie was eager to get to church so she could practice a bit before the service started. Ruth and Eugene were electrified. This was the night that Santa paid his yearly visit. Sitting in the car, waiting for Amanda to emerge from the house, they echoed their thoughts on what Santa would bring. Finally Amanda was seated in the car. Buster left his dog house, wagging his tail and barking as they drove away. He gave one big lunge and the chain snapped from the dog house. He was free.

Soon, excited children, with parents in tow, arrived for this special night. Tootie was at the organ ready for the order of events. She started a medley of Christmas songs. People were still filing in, finding seats. The ushers were setting up additional seating. Paul, with his vestments on, was ready to greet his flock. The Niedlichs were seated near the back.

A great commotion near the rear caused Herb and Amanda to turn their heads. Buster, chain dragging behind him, trotted down the aisle making his way to the Christmas tree. Amanda, utterly embarrassed, hid her face from view. Herb quickly got up, retrieved the vagabond dog just before he had a chance to tangle with the tree. Herb, somewhat amused, shook his head as he hurried the dog out. Driving Buster home, he was secured in the garage for the time being. Herb hurried back to church, the program already being in progress. The children had sung their opening song.

One small boy in the front row was entertaining the congregation. He kept elbowing the girl next to him. Then he took off his tie and stuffed it in his pocket, bent down and retied his shoes. Amanda looked at the boy's mother who was hiding her face in her hands. People were quietly laughing behind cupped hands at the antics of this young one.

The program over, happy faces on the congeners, they earnestly greeted their friends and neighbors with, "Merry Christmas!" Excitement

prevailed all around.

Along with the Sunday School children, the children in the audience also received a sack of goodies. Reverend Riech greeted each one of the members and visitors at the door. They quickly spoke their greetings and then hurried their children home.

Martin and Laura stayed a bit after the service to pick up papers, straightening the hymnals and what ever else needed attention for the next day's service. Rose, too, assisted to get things in proper order. She was yearning to hurry on home. Patience was not a noticeable virtue for her on this evening. She had hopes that the night would hold wonderful mysteries for her.

As they drove home, the outside lights of several homes and that of the town itself, made the Abends heart warm with praise to God—this the most wonderful night of the year! Rose had other reasons to feel the warmth of this night.

They hurried to their home. Rose, rushing in ahead, turned on the Christmas tree lights. Laura went into the kitchen to get some coffee brewing, setting out a plate full of her Christmas cookies as well. As Martin entered the house they all gathered around the tree. Opening Christmas gifts was their order for the evening.

No sooner had they finished opening gifts when there was a knock at the door. Rose jumped up and quickly hastened to the door. Mary, Joe's sister, was on the other side. She whispered, "Joe is home. Can you come?"

Rose invited her in and then went to tell her parents that she wanted to go over to Mary's.

"On this special night, Rose?" her father asked.

"Please let me go for awhile Dad. I have a gift for Mary and she has one for me."

"Okay," her father disappointingly said. "Don't stay too long. We have church tomorrow morning."

"I will be home soon."

Scarves tightly wound around their necks, snow crunching beneath their feet, they hastened to the Caridin home. Rose was totally a case of jitters.

As they virtually ran, Mary said, "Mom and Dad already know that the two of you want to get married."

"Well, that's one down. Now for me to get up enough nerve to tell my folks."

With a bit of a wind in the air, making it rather difficult to talk as they hurried along, no other words were spoken.

Approaching the front door, Mary allowed Rose to enter first. Proceeding into the house her eyes caught sight of the beautifully decorated Christmas tree first. Glancing toward the side, she saw Joe standing beside it. Her heart did several flip flops and all she could do was gaze at him. He hurried across the room to her and scooped her up into his arms, almost squeezing the life out of her, giving her a long overdue, lingering kiss. He set her feet back on the floor, looking into her beautiful blue eyes, he said, "I'm so in love with you."

Beaming a brilliant smile, eyes sparkling as she gazed into his eyes, she said, "I've missed you so much, Joe." Planting a kiss upon his lips, he held her firmly.

After she removed her overshoes, Joe, taking her hand, pulled her beside the tree. She greeted the rest of the family. Lois, Joe's mother, went to the kitchen to bring in some treats. A gift exchange followed.

Joe was the eldest of the siblings, then Mary, followed by James, Margret, Andy and Ann. Joe had brought gifts for all of them.

Pete, Joe's father, said, "If you're planning on getting married, Joe, you should have saved your money instead of buying all these gifts."

"You are probably right—but I just wanted this to be a special Christmas, Dad."

Joe and Rose were seated on the couch, he had his arm around her shoulder. The gift that he had bought for her was a beautiful gold plated broach fashioned into a rose. Uttering her oohs and aahs, she immediately took it from the box and started to pin it on her blue pull over sweater, which she was wearing with a white and blue plaid pleated skirt.

Joe interrupted her saying, "Here, allow me." He took the pin, pinned it on her sweater saying, "A golden rose for my beautiful Rose."

She, smiling at him, voiced, "Why thank you, Joe! You're so romantic." She kissed him.

He whispered in her ear, "Do you think that you could go to the midnight mass with us?"

"Joe, there is nothing that I would rather do but I better get back to my family."

"Will you please tell them about us very soon."

"I'll tell them before New Years Day."

"That's not soon enough for me, but I guess it will have to be. Come on, I'll give you a ride home." Then he said, "Dad, I'll warm up the car for us as I take Rose home. Is that okay?"

"Sure, son, go right ahead."

The two love birds exited the house and got into the cold car. As they waited for the car to warm up, Joe was getting his long overdue kisses. They had a lot to talk about. What was Joe going to do now that he was finally home? When would they be getting married? Whose church would they be married in? Where would they live? So went their conversation.

As they parked in front of Rose's home, Joe pulled her into his arms and said, "I'm so happy to be home, so happy to have you in my arms again! What a wonderful Christmas!"

"I've prayed so hard for you to come home in one piece, Joe. I'm glad that all of you came home to me and not just part of you. I'm so in love with you."

"I'm going to walk you to the door, Rose. If your family sees us, then so be it."

They walked to the door, Joe kissed her good night and said, "Please come by tomorrow."

"I'll be over in the afternoon."

He waited until she had entered the house and then drove home.

Chapter Eleven

With an effulgently dressed Christmas tree, giving its beams of color to the living room, and a house beautifully decorated with a distinct display of the Christ Child's birth, Amanda was hustling about readying things for Christmas dinner. Arising early, she had the dinning room table covered with a white linen cloth that had Christmas trees embroidered in each corner. Her best dishes were set upon it. A Christmas arrangement, that she had made out of evergreen branches and candles, was placed in the middle of the table. Potatoes were peeled and placed in cold water. As Tamar entered the kitchen, Amanda was preparing the two geese. Tamar helped her with the two types of dressing—apple/raisin and sauerkraut. Carl and Sophia along with Margie and Rufus and the Becks, would be their guests for dinner. Amanda and Tamar hurried along with their chores. Tamar was the organist for this day and it was imperative that they arrive at church in time for her to run through the hymns before church started.

Margie, being employed in a defense plant in Fort Wayne, was able to get time off to celebrate Christmas with her family in Anderville. Now that the war was over she was afraid that soon her job would be terminated. She had other plans if that was to take place.

The Christmas Eve Service had quelled the prospect of a cardinal need for some members to attend the worship service at St. Peter's on Christmas Day. Yet the church was reasonably filled. Reverend Riech had prepared a meaningful message and an all over service. The choir had offered a beautiful arrangement selected from one of Handel's pieces

taken from his Messiah. It was well received with the congregators wanting to rise and clap as they finished. The duet performed by Paul and Martin, was also a great addition to the service. Many of the members extended their thanks to Paul for including the duet in the worship service. Before the service and after it, people were greeting one another with happy voices and happy faces. This was a good Christmas, the war was over and a few of the soldiers had already returned home and would be enjoying the holidays with their loved ones.

Maxine was in attendance but didn't bother Paul other than to wish him a Merry Christmas and a safe trip to Milwaukee. She handed him a jar of peach preserves that she had made, the gift tastefully wrapped in gold cellophane paper and tied with green ribbon. He thanked her graciously, wondering if he had finally succeeded in breaking her motivation. That would indeed be a godsend, he felt.

The Niedlichs, the Becks and Sophia and Carl Platz, along with Margie and Rufus, greeted him, wishing him a very Merry Christmas. Each of the families had a gift for him. Amanda had made some Pfeffernusse, a small hard cookie to be dunked in coffee, for him and had attached a gift of money as well. Dorthea and Bill's gift was homemade smoked summer sausage and a gift of money. Sophia and Carl, having raised ten children, had a difficult time coming up with a monetary gift. They were constrained to frugal living every month. They presented him with a jar of sweet pickles and a jar of apricots that she had canned. He appeared very pleased to receive all of their gifts and thanked them all profoundly.

The last of the members having left the building, Paul removed his robe, cleared his desk, put on his topcoat and left for Milwaukee. His mother had phoned him on Christmas Eve after he had returned from the church service, and enlightened him with the fact that his sister and husband and children had arrived on that afternoon. He was eager to see them.

The Abends had invited Mrs. Oberling for dinner. The entire family went and picked her up, escorting her to the worship service with them, taking her to their home afterward. The dinner and visiting went well. Mary Oberling, very pleased to have a day out, was revealing past Christmas experiences. One of them that she imparted to them was about

her daughter, now living in Chicago with a large family of her own.

"She was her papa's girl," she divulged. "Always the tomboy. When she was twelve years old she wanted a rifle for Christmas. Her father and I talked it over and finally bought her a second hand one. I had hidden it under the couch in the living room. Having gifts to put out for all the children on Christmas Eve, I forgot to take the rifle from its hiding place. Christmas morning all of the children had a gift and there wasn't anything for Marie. We could see that she was very disappointed but was trying so hard not to cry. Feeling badly for her, August got his foot to working under the couch so as not to be noticeable to the children, shifted it about so that it was partially showing. One of the other children saw it and asked, 'Why did Santa put that under the couch?' Well you can bet that there was one happy girl!"

"Did she ever shoot anything with it?" Warren, the youngest Abends boy, asked.

"She did indeed. Going hunting with her father was a big treat for her."

They talked on about other happenings which involved things that her deceased husband, August, had witnessed as a boy. The children were struck with awe as she unraveled the tale of August seeing a ghost—a headless white horse running around a well and then disappearing. Mary held their attention with her episodes of long ago.

After they finished their dessert of apple and pumpkin pie, Laura insisted that Mary Oberling relax in the living room and visit with Martin while she and Rose did the dishes. The boys, too, found seats so that they could listen to more of her tales.

Dinner dishes cleaned and put away, Rose asked to be excused. Of course she had her mind set on seeing Joe.

Wrapped warmly in her tweed coat, she hurried over to the Caridin home. This situation of keeping secrets from her parents, racked her mind. How could she get it out in the open? Yet she had no idea how to reveal this guise. *I'll wait until the reverend returns from Milwaukee and I'll talk to him about this,* was her choice in the matter.

The Niedlichs home was filled with much laughter, Dorthea always saw to that. She was teasing Tamar about getting herself a beau.

"Well, there is a nice looking young man that I talk to quite often. He's going to be a teacher. He really wants to be a minister but that takes more years of schooling and he doesn't have the money. He decided to be a teacher instead. I like talking with him."

"You'll have to bring him home some weekend and let us check him out. We'll let you know if we think he'd make a good husband for you."

Tamar answered, "I'd be afraid of what all of you would confront him with."

Dorthea laughed and said, "We would never embarrass you."

"For some reason I don't quite believe you," she replied.

Everyone laughed and other conversation went on. Margie was talking to Rufus about going back to Fort Wayne with her on Wesnesday morning.

Grandma announced, "Well maybe I'll go with you and visit Ruth and her family. I'll get to visit with Rufus a little more that way, too."

"That's a good idea, Ma," Margie said. "Pa, don't you want to come along too?"

"No, I'll stay home and keep the home fires burning. Rufus will surely visit us soon anyway."

So it was decided.

Rose, arriving at the Caridin home, was sweetly welcomed into Joe's arms.

He hugged her tenderly and then said, "Come on, I want to show you something."

He ushered her out of the house and to the family car.

"Where are we going?" Rose inquired.

"You'll see."

He drove out directly north of town on a gravel road. He kept smiling and winking at her, enjoying the puzzled look that he had put on her face.

Five-miles out of town, Joe pulled into a driveway that was lined with white birch trees.

"What are we going to do here?" she asked.

He stopped the car, put his arm around her, gave her a kiss and with a twinkle in his eyes, asked, "How would you like to live here?"

"Do you mean that we can?"

"Well, good friends of our family own this. He has made me a good offer to buy it. Maybe with a G. I. loan we would be able to do that."

The house in question was on a farm. It had been built for hired help to live in. Not in need of a hired man anymore the house was for sale.

"Can we see the inside?"

"I just thought that you might want to. I picked up the key after church this morning."

They broke through the snow making a path to the front door. Joe opened the door for them. It was very tidy and bright inside. Taking Rose's hand, Joe pulled her from room to room as they moved about. There was a good sized master bedroom, two smaller bedrooms, a small but adequate bathroom, a good sized living room, a kitchen big enough to feed an army. The back porch was enclosed. And a basement, along with all of this, was a good selling point. The sun shone through the kitchen windows making the home very inviting.

"How do you like it?" he asked.

"Its beautiful!"

"I thought that you might be thrilled with it."

"You're going to have to find work first, aren't you?"

"I'll start looking tomorrow."

"Well, I'll keep on working too."

"For now maybe, but not forever."

"I'd love to live here!"

"See, there's some land that goes with it, too. We can raise chickens—maybe pigs."

Their conversation continued as they returned to the Caridin home. Of course, Joe was always asking Rose if she had revealed to her folks the fact that they were going to be married.

Preparing for bed that evening, Rose was so excited about all that was happening. She felt an urge to share all aspects of this part of her life with her mother. However, she didn't want to spring any unhappiness on them during this Christmas season. She prayed that God would send an opening.

On Friday Paul returned to Anderville. Having had a very pleasant visit with his family he was eager to get back to his flock. Playing with his niece and nephews incited a yearning for a family of his own. He did talk to his family about Vivian. They listened intensely and then suggested that it probably wouldn't be a good idea to pursue his interest in Vivian. After a moments thought Paul readily agreed, saying that now his life was earmarked for Christ.

He stopped at the drug store to pick up the town's weekly paper on his way into town. Rose was working and smiled brightly as he walked up to the counter.

"Hello, Rose," he happily voiced.

"Hi Reverend Riech. How were things in Milwaukee?"

"It was great! I had a marvelous time."

"Well, it's good to have you back."

"It's pleasant to have a break from routine but always good to return home."

Thinking for a brief second, she then asked, "Reverend, do you think that you could squeeze in some time for me? I'm in a dither about a perplexing problem."

"Of course, Rose. I could see you tomorrow, maybe even this evening if it's urgent."

"Well, it is rather urgent but it can wait until morning."

"Okay. I'll see you at 9:00 tomorrow morning."

He picked up his paper, said his adieus and left.

Not able to live a day without the sight of Rose, Joe often visited the pharmacy. He wondered how he had lived through war time without her. Since no one knew about their involvement except his family, they both kept a low profile. Although it was hard to rein in her emotions, to Rose he was just another customer. Art Simpson often pondered on the reason that Joe visited the pharmacy on more than one occasion in a days time.

Saturday morning Rose was up early. Neatly dressed for work, she walked to the Caridin's. Joe was waiting for her and gave her a ride to the church. Butterflies were rampant in her stomach, making her very jittery.

"Calm down, Rose. No one is going to eat you."

"I know. I really should be able to take care of this myself without

involving Reverend Riech."

"It's all right to talk with him. Eventually we'd have to anyway. Do you want me to go in with you?"

"Maybe you should, since this includes you too."

Paul was surprised to see a young man escorting Rose into the building. She adhered to the moment and introduced Joe to him.

"I'm very pleased to meet you, Joe."

He invited them to be seated and although he had a slight notion of what this was about he asked anyway, "And how can I help you this morning?"

"Rose and I are very much in love. Because of a difference in our religious background she is afraid to tell her parents that we want to get married. I'm Catholic, you see. I know that I should ask for Rose's hand in marriage, but her parents don't even have a clue that we have been seeing each other, even before I left for the navy."

Rose added, " I don't want to disappoint them and don't really know how to tell them."

"Well, this is a bit of a surprise." He thought for a moment, and then said, "As I see it Rose, your parents will be disappointed, but I'm sure that they won't disown you. You must tell them. That's the only way to get this out in the open. There are other issues that must be confronted here as well. Have the two of you discussed which church you are going to be associated with and where your children will be baptized and where they will go to church? I'm well aware of the fact that the Catholic church holds its own."

"We have talked about it," Rose answered, "and have decided to continue in our own faith for the time being. When we have children we'll decide what to do about their Christian upbringing then."

"This is something that you absolutely should resolve before you get married. It can cause too much conflict later."

"I am so in love with Joe and I want to make a good wife for him and a good marriage. I don't want to live a life without him."

"I understand how you two feel about this. I too, was smitten with a Catholic girl once. But my situation is different from yours. All that I ask you two to do is pray together about this."

"I respect Rose's beliefs," Joe inserted, "and have agreed to have the wedding here. We certainly will pray about these other matters. We want to have a godly home."

"That's very admirable of the both of you."

They went on talking until it was time for Rose to leave for work. Joe shook hands with the Reverend. Paul invited them to come anytime to talk with him. Their departure left a host of questions that still needed answers.

Paul sat back in his chair, hands locked behind his head, contemplating about all of the complications religion plays into the lives of lovers. *Why does it have to be that way?* He frowned. *Our goal is the same. Each one of us is proceeding toward Heaven. Christ said that we only have to believe in the merits of his body and blood and be baptized to be saved. The Catholics believe in Christ's merits and they also baptize. Why is this so difficult?* He thought that a portion of it, in fact most of it, was in the way people had been raised. Bowing his head, he earnestly prayed for Joe and Rose.

Chapter Twelve

As he said he would, Joe started pounding the streets looking for work the day after Christmas. This detail generated both pain and pleasure; the pain instituted by the "no work to be had here" announcement; pleasure being derived from the fact that he was back home and, also, he had received a few "maybes." He felt that in a few months the farmers would be needing help and if nothing came through he would hire out to a farmer. Because they wanted to get married right away this idea went against his constitution. *Maybe I'll go to Hutchinson and see if there is any work there,* he thought. Since the town was bigger than Anderville it could accommodate some of the unemployed, he felt. Everyone that he spoke to was very touched by his need for work. After all, these boys had been away fighting a war and now they needed to be paired with a job.

He walked to the drug store. Rose waited on him properly and he quietly asked her to walk to the Caridin home after work.

She was agreeable and said, "I'll call Mom and tell her that I'm meeting Mary after work and won't be home until late."

Walking home, Joe, knowing that he had some money saved, was still mindful of the reality that he needed full time employment before they could marry. He was, nevertheless, perplexed about the job market in Anderville.

Rose hastily cleaned the counters and straightened chairs, tidying up everything as her shift ended. Putting on her overshoes, coat and stocking cap, picking up her purse, she voiced a good night to Art Simpson and hurried along to the Caridins.

Anxiously waiting for her, Joe met her at the door, hugged her, placed

a kiss upon her lips, and led her to the sofa. They commiserated on the job situation.

"We can't get married until I get a job," he announced to Rose.

Since Rose had not worked up the nerve to tell her parents yet, she wasn't too unhappy with that statement.

"Maybe we'll have to move somewhere where there is work," he thoughtfully uttered.

"I hate to leave Anderville and my job," Rose responded.

"I know. I hate to leave here too. Maybe we need to pray about it a lot more."

They sat, Joe with his arm around Rose, thinking about their predicament.

"Surely something will come up soon," Rose speculated.

"I was so in hopes that we could be married soon," Joe articulated. He continued with, "Let's go and get a hamburger in Hutchinson and ask around about the job situation there."

"Good idea!"

They left in Joe's dad's car.

It was getting on towards New Year's and as yet, Rose had not told her parents about Joe. Joe kept reminding her that she'd have to do it soon.

Asking about the job opportunities in Hutchinson, they were numbed by the fact that there wasn't much there either, especially in the realm of work that Joe wanted. Their travel back to Anderville was bitter sweet.

With alcoholic based drinks in hand, a host of Anderville citizens were celebrating the end of a year. Some of the Irish Catholics were very eager celebrators, what with the war being over and all. And of course, some of the Lutherans felt that it was a time for celebration as well.

For New Year's Eve the Niedlichs opted for a "singsperation" and had invited Reverend Riech, also. Amanda had prepared some mouth watering food. Without Grandma around, Grandpa was a bit at a loss. He arrived earlier at the Niedlich home and enjoyed visiting with the family. The Becks came after they had their chores finished.

Everyone was ready to sample Amanda's delectable food. Reverend Riech's arrival not a positive yet, prompted Amanda to keep the food

warm in the warming oven.

"Are you sure that he is coming?" Dorthea asked.

"I'm sure that he will be here. Something must have happened to keep him."

Meanwhile, in the other part of town, Luella Erst had arrived home from her day's work at Doctor Jeffery's. Going in through the back door of her home she noticed Tom's body prostrate at the foot of the basement steps. He wasn't moving. With a foreboding feeling in her heart she descended the stairs. "Tom, Tom," she called. He didn't move. She could smell the liqueur on his clothes. Touching him he felt very cold. Their son, Lewis, was out delivering goods for one of the stores. Not having a phone in their home and unable to rely on Lewis, she hastened to the neighbors to call for help.

Her neighbor, Mrs. Evans, said, "Oh dear. Come sit down, I'll phone for you."

She phoned the respective authorities and then asked Luella if she would like her to phone Reverend Riech. Luella, emotionally distressed, nodded.

Mrs. Evans walked with Luella to her home just as the authorities arrived. Paul reached her home soon after.

The medics could find no pulse on Tom. Conferring with Luella and Reverend Riech, they took necessary steps to remove the body from the residence. It appeared that Tom had over indulged, lost his balance, fell down the steps and broke his neck. Luella sobbed for her mate. Paul, making mental images that this could be a relative of his but by God's grace, put his arms around her and tried to comfort her.

"It's good to cry, Luella. Just let the tears fall. You know the story, I'm sure, of how Jesus cried for his friends Mary and Martha after their brother died. We, too, cry with you Luella." He let her cry on his shoulder.

Mrs. Evans was stunned at this senseless death but was so moved at how Reverend Riech was handling the situation. Bernice Evans and her husband Bernard were amongst the unchurched. They, however, were very good neighbors to the Erst family.

After Luella quieted down, Paul prepared to leave saying that he would

be in touch with her the next day. He had prayed with her, had even waited until Lewis came home to be with her.

Arriving at the Niedlich home a half hour late, he explained to them the situation surrounding his tardiness. Hearts filled with empathy for Luella and Lewis, they murmured their shock. That incident put a bit of a damper in the festive mood for the evening. Everyone rose above it though, and the singing was heartwarming.

When the Niedlichs were made aware of the fact that their minister played the saxophone, they had asked him to bring it along to be included in some instrumental music as well. With Tamar at the organ, Paul on his saxophone, Herb on his violin, the house fairly shook with musical vibrations. John had received a guitar for Christmas. Just learning how to play it, he would enter into the joyous music wherever he could. Bill clapped with the music, then grabbed Dorthea and danced her around the room. She patted her stomach after the music stopped and laughing away said, "Well, this is the first dance this little one has had." The others joined her laughter.

Paul wanted very much to start a conversation with Tamar. He witnessed her smile which was almost hypnotic, along with her pretty dimples.

"Are you staying at the dormitory?" he started.

"No. Another gal and I rent a private room not far from the college."

"Maybe I could stop to see how you are doing when I go to St. Paul to pick up supplies," he offered.

Tamar was a bit hesitant in answering. To her, Paul was nothing more than her minister. She had never envisioned him as a suitor. But then, maybe he was only being protective.

She then answered, "You're welcome to stop by and see how I am faring."

The evening drew to a close and everyone with a good time tucked into their memory bank, left for home. Paul took hold of Tamar's hand, which felt so small within his larger one. He placed his other hand on top of them and said, "It was a very fine evening. I'll see you at church in the morning."

"It surely was a fun and safe way to spend New Year's Eve. I'll see you

in the morning." She smiled her prettiest and said, "Goodbye."

Paul thanked Amanda and Herb whole heartily and said his goodbyes to the rest.

At church the next morning, Paul's sermon, "Striving Our Best To Follow Our Savior In The New Year," had his congregators taking inventory of their spiritual needs. His sermon was well laid out. During the announcements he disclosed that Tom Erst had died and the funeral was pending. There were more than a few murmurs in the audience. After the service he asked Tootie to play for the burial. She was a bit apprehensive since she, as yet, had not played for a funeral service. He encouraged her and she finally accepted the challenge.

Maxine again waited to be the last one to shake hands with Paul.

As Tamar walked up to Paul, she smiled and said, "Thank you for that justly deserved admonition for our walk with Christ in this New Year."

"You're welcome, Tamar. So you're off to St. Paul this afternoon?"

"Yes. It's time to get my mind back on my studies."

"I'll soon be going to St. Paul and I'll look you up. Can you wait a few minutes so that I can take down your address?"

"Sure, I'll wait."

Maxine tuned up her hearing senses in hopes of enlightening herself with what Reverend Riech was saying to Tamar.

Walking over to Maxine, Paul extended his hand and said, "You'll be leaving for school soon, too, I understand."

"Yes, I'm leaving this afternoon. I'll be home Friday evening. Reverend, a bunch of the Youth League kids are going ice skating this coming Saturday evening. I wondered if you'd like to go with me?"

"I'm unaware that there is going to be an ice skating party."

"Oh, it's not the Youth League assembly, it's just some of us that got it together. I hope that you can go with me?"

"I'm not sure what's going on this week. If I am able to attend I'll drive over by myself. I might need the car to get to an ill parishioner."

That wasn't exactly how she had it planned. She was disappointed. Noticing his interest in Tamar didn't set too well with her either. She thought, *first that librarian and now Tamar. Do I have to knock him over the head*

to get him to pay attention to me!

She watched as Tamar and Paul headed for his office. Again her feathers were ruffled. Dejected, she walked to the Schmit's car.

Paul and Tamar talked a bit about the funeral service that was coming up. Music took over some of their conversation, also.

"I enjoyed the music immensely last evening," Paul injected.

"It was very heart warming. Maybe we can have another one around Easter time."

"I'll not throw cold water on that idea. That would be great!"

"We'll have to schedule that for this spring," Tamar said.

As Tamar gave him her address and phone number, he said, "I'll miss your gentle spirit."

"Well, thank you, Reverend."

They said their goodbyes.

Going to see Luella and Lewis after church, his heart was heavy for them. The two, although still stunned by the departure of Tom, had accepted his death. They had decided on the funeral service for Friday morning. Paul prayed with them again and then gave Luella a sympathetic hug. Remembering how his minister had aided him when his own father died, Paul took hold of Lewis shoulders, saying, "If there is ever anything that you need to know or need help with, please, please feel free to come to me." Lewis, hands in his pockets, just looked at him and nodded. He was a rather quiet individual.

This would be Paul's first burial service. With his sensitive heart, he prayed fervently for God's presence in this matter. *It's all right to weep with the family,* Paul thought, *Jesus wept too. I just don't want to break down during the service though. That wouldn't be very proper.* He had an inner recognition that his Maker would properly see him through the ordeal.

Rose, hearing the news at church that morning, felt stricken with the incident but couldn't wait to get home, wanting nothing more than to run over to Joe's to tell him of the tragedy.

After the dinner dishes were cleaned and put away, Rose asked to be excused and hurried to the Caridins as fast as her legs would carry her.

Joe met her at the door. She fairly flew into their house saying, "Joe, Joe, Tom Erst died. He worked for the lumber company. Maybe you can

get his job!"

He took hold of her shoulders, looking into her very blue eyes, said, "Slow down, slow down. I heard about that after I dropped you off last night. I'm going over to the lumber company first thing tomorrow morning. Real early. We'll pray that I get the job. This means that you best be telling your folks about us."

"I will tell them today."

Excitement reigned in the hearts of the two love birds. They had lots to discuss. If all went well with the lumber company, they planned on being married on Valentine's Day.

Joe, in his exuberance, picked up Rose and swung her about. She was thoroughly washed with happiness.

"Mary, you will make a very lovely maid of honor," she exclaimed.

"You know, I'll be so proud being your maid of honor!"

More discourse went on about the wedding. What time of the day would the wedding take place? What would be Rose's choice in colors for the wedding? She chose red and white. Who would be in charge of the reception? With every question that had an answer, Joe placed a kiss upon her lips, declaring, "Another hatchet buried."

Chapter Thirteen

Everything was looking and smelling like roses for Joe and his bride to be. He was able to obtain the job at the lumber company but only for part time work. However, Justin Hammer, who interviewed Joe, suggested that with the war being over, young men coming home from the war front, more homes would have to be built. He was sure that in a short time Joe would be employed full time. They had another employee, Samuel Schwartz, who was a full time worker. Joe was satisfied with this. His plan was to hire out to farmers whenever he could. They had other good news as well. The Shay family, owners of the house that Rose and Joe had looked at, offered it to them to rent while they waited for their loan to go through. Rose couldn't believe their good fortune.

On this day after New year's, Rose was a guest at the Caridins that evening. Joe finally got up the nerve and said, "Rose, we are going to your house and we are going to talk to your folks and I will tell them of my intentions and will ask for your hand in marriage."

A bit surprised at his statement, Rose was willing to go along with his plan. Putting on their winter wraps, they left.

Martin and Laura were sitting in their easy chairs in the living room when Joe and Rose entered the house. Slightly bewildered to see the two together, surprise registered in their eyes and question marks appeared on their faces.

Rose began with, "Mom and Dad, there is something that I should have told you a long time ago." She took a deep breath and continued with, "Joe and I are in love and have been for three years."

"You don't say," her father replied.

"I know that it wasn't right for me to keep this from you but I knew that because Joe is Catholic, you'd be unhappy about our involvement."

"Well…I am shocked," her mother said, and went on with, "Am I so far estranged from you that you couldn't confide in me, Rose?"

"No, Mom. I'm sorry. I know that I should have told you."

Martin with a heavy heart asked, "And haven't I always been a reliable person to bring your hopes and dreams to?"

"Yes, Dad, you have been. I'm very sorry to have disappointed both of you. Can you please forgive me and give us your blessing for our marriage?"

Joe walked up to Martin and said, "Mr. Abends, I would be the happiest man in the world if you would consent to give me your daughter's hand in marriage."

"Wait a minute, wait just a minute. Things are moving too fast here. There are things to discuss before I agree to this. You might as well take a chair."

They both sat down on the sofa, Joe holding Rose's hand.

"Just how do you propose to meet the needs of our daughter and yourself, Joe?"

"I'm sorry. We should have explained first that I have part time work at the lumber company here in town and I'll work for some of the farmers too. Mr. Hammer said he was positive that the job would soon be full time. We already have a place to live."

Martin and Laura, although disappointed, were relieved to hear that. They went on telling Rose's parents that the wedding would be held at St. Peter's, also mentioning that they had already talked to Reverend Riech. With their hearts still filled with frustration, they did consent to the marriage.

Rose hugged both of her parents, thanking them for making her the happiest girl in the entire world. Joe shook hands with Martin and said, "I'll never give you reason to regret that you gave me Rose's hand."

"I trust that you will keep that promise."

Martin had taught Joe in high school and he knew him to be an outstanding young man. Martin surmised that most of his own ill feelings

came from the fact that he was losing his lovely daughter.

As they were leaving Rose said, "I'll be home early and maybe we can make plans for the reception."

"I'd appreciate that Rose. There is a lot to decide on."

The happy couple fairly skipped to the car, hands locked together and glad that this ordeal was over. They left to play cards with Joe's siblings.

The next day Joe had his first day of work. He was full of energy and worked tirelessly. His main thought was, *I now have a wife to support, I'll work hard for her.*

Wanting to purchase a car, at the noontime break he talked to the full-time employee, Samuel Schwartz, about his need.

"My grandfather has a 1937 Plymouth for sale. It's a good car. He's just too old to drive it."

Joe was interested. Samuel gave him their address. Joe's idea was to go there after work to look it over.

Rose was on a cloud. She and Laura had discussed wedding plans when she arrived home from the Caridins the evening after New Year's Day. Being very energized, Rose already had concrete plans for most of the affair. They talked about furniture for their home.

"Mom, I'm so in love that I'd eat off of a plank across two saw horses and sit on apple crates."

"Well, I guess that's one way of getting started. It would be nice if you'd wait awhile to start a family."

"That's not always an option, Mom. Remember, he's Catholic."

"I guess, even though Joe is a nice young man, I'll always wish that you had married in your own faith."

"You don't know what God may have in store for us, Mom."

She hugged her mother.

Phoning Reverend Reich before she left for work the next day, Rose had secured February 14th, at 6:30 in the evening, for their wedding. She also mentioned her desire to have Tamar play for the wedding. He gave Rose her phone number.

Now that the partnership of Joe and Rose was a known factor, Rose

didn't have to hide the situation anymore. She enthusiastically talked to those she worked with about the upcoming wedding.

Joe's thoughts that evening, as he was driving to pick up Rose from work with the car that he had purchased from Samuel's grandfather, were, *This is so much easier now that Rose's parents know about us.* The car handled great and Joe was exhilarated. Art Simpson noticed the change in Joe's manner as he entered the pharmacy. He congratulated him and small talk ensued. A customer walked in. Art patted Joe on the shoulder and strolled away to help the patron.

Holding the door open for Rose as they left the drug store, he led her to the Plymouth. She was pleasantly surprised at the fact that Joe had acquired a car.

"I'm giving you fair warning, Rose, you'll have to learn how to drive it."

"Oh yes! I want to be able to drive!" she excitedly remarked.

They spun away to get a sandwich and then the two went out to their home-to-be, stopping first at the Shay's farm to pay their first month's rent. Mr. Shay allowed them free rent for the rest of January, starting their obligation for the first of February. They wouldn't actually be living there until the 14th but they needed to have access so that they could set up for housekeeping. There were windows that needed to be measured, curtains to be made for them and linoleum or carpets to be laid. Rose knew that she would be one busy person.

Joe insisted, "Don't forget me, Rose. I want to help too."

"Don't worry, you'll get your share of work," she said as she gave him a hug.

"You're not getting by with just a hug," he said, and pulled her to him for a kiss.

That same day Martin went to visit his friend, Paul Riech. Paul gladly received him. Of course their discussions were mainly about Martin's injured feelings. Paul sympathized with him, also suggesting the plus side of the issue.

"Yes," Martin volunteered, "I should be happy for her. They don't come much better than Joe. He's very respectful and treats his family well.

He's very intelligent too. I guess I had always hoped that she would go to college and meet a nice man with a college degree."

"Certainly, I give you that thought. Well, let's pray about it and hope that he'll make a good living for his family. I myself believe that the key to this entire relationship is that in their own way, they each want a Christian home. Joe himself told me that."

"You are right. I should be thankful for that."

Martin left Paul's office feeling much better about his daughter's choice.

The skies poured down measures of its contents on those who attended the funeral of Tom Erst. Some of the people in town thought, *just as he lived, drunken and cantankerous, the skies are obliging him with their wrath.*

Paul, wanting to send rays of hope to the mourners, prepared a comforting service. Martin Abends sang, "Abide With Me and The Lords Prayer." Tootie stationed at the organ, did very well. Of course she had to miss a bit of school to adhere to this duty. Paul also felt that he had been visited by a heavenly angel. He breezed through the service without a hitch.

Amidst traces of snow and wind, Tom was laid to rest. He was only forty-nine years old. There was much sadness. Paul comforted Lewis and Luella.

The ladies of the church had set out tasty food. Amanda and Dorthea were among the workers. Sophia, too, was able to help. She had returned from Indiana by bus the day after New year's.

After the luncheon was over, Paul talked to Luella, again offering comforting words. He also made sure that Lewis understood his availability to talk at anytime.

People leaving to go home, the men folk shoveled snow away from the church steps, sidewalk and around vehicles. Dorthea and Dorene were situated in their Model T. Dorthea started the car, backing it over a small mound of snow. Just then a crawly substance around her feet, issued forth a scream as Dorthea opened the door and jumped out. A mouse followed her out. She screamed again. Amanda, noticing that her sister was in trouble, went to see if she could assist.

"Are you okay?" she asked.

"There was a mouse in our car," Dorthea answered.

Amanda, remembering an old wives tale, asked, "You didn't touch yourself anywhere did you?"

"Oh...I don't think so. It just scared the life out of me. That's what happens when we use this car to carry feed in."

Amanda recalled a nice looking lady she had known years ago, who had a birthmark the size of a quarter on her face that looked like mouse skin. It was said that her mother had touched her face when she became frightened by a mouse, when she was pregnant with her. Amanda wasn't sure if there was any truth to it but she felt that it might be so.

Everything in a settled state once more, the two ladies departed for home, Amanda giving her mother a ride home.

On Saturday night, the big night of the skating party, Paul thought that he would attend the gathering for a short time. He wasn't planning on skating. Rose had also been invited and she and Joe were present. There were other young girls there, some without partners. A few of the young men just home from the war zone, were also invited by those who were in charge.

Maxine, noticing Paul standing on the side line, skated up to him and said, "How about a skate?"

"Hello Maxine. I just stopped by for a minute."

He was actually hoping that she would hook up with one of the soldiers that had just returned from the war. He could see that some of the young men, some he didn't even recognize, were not from his parish.

"Why don't we just watch then and talk a bit." She started taking off her skates, continuing with, "I'll get us some hot cocoa."

There was a building near the skating rink that was heated. Walking over to it Maxine got two cups of the hot treat. Paul took a seat on one of the benches and watched the skaters. Maxine hurried back, her hands balancing two cups of hot cocoa.

No sooner had she sat down than a young man skated over and asked her for the next skate.

"I don't think...."

Paul interrupted her saying, "Maxine, I have to leave. You go ahead and skate. I have a house call to make this evening."

The young man was nice looking with a height not equal to Paul's, but not a short man either. He was slender and had green eyes. Maxine recognized him from high school. He had graduated three years ahead of her. She quickly put on her skates, said goodbye to Paul and skated away with her would-be pursuer.

Finishing his hot cocoa, Paul left and drove toward Vivian's home. He had phoned her before he left for the skating party, expressing his intentions to stop by.

Vivian, dressed in a ruffled white blouse and red plaid pleated skirt, met him at the door with her delightful smile.

He entered and she directed him to her charming living room. Seating himself on an upholstered chair, he was reluctant to say what he knew needed to be said.

"You have your home nicely decorated," he began.

"Jim and I bought most of the things. I added some things later."

"It's very pleasing to the eye."

Taking a deep breath he started with, "Vivian, I wish that things were different for us. I have very much enjoyed our times together."

"I have enjoyed your company as well."

"You understand that if things were different, I'd be the first one at your door to court you properly. Since my profession stands in the way, it's best that I stick to my goals. I'll be visiting the library from time to time for books and for references, though. I know that I will be the one that is most injured by my decision. I needed to tell you before your heart got too engaged in our friendship. And if by my actions in your presence I have in anyway given you false hope, I apologize. Please forgive me if so."

Paul looking into Vivian's eyes, knew that he had just sent an arrow through her heart. He felt badly.

She, however rose to the occasion and said, " I understand your situation, Paul. Isn't there some way that this could work?"

"Vivian, I really think that it's best for both of us to find someone in our own faith. It's not that it couldn't work in another town. Here in Anderville it just won't work."

"I understand although I don't want to."

"I'll always be your friend Vivian, and of course I'll still be stopping by for books."

"I, too, wish that it could be different. I'll be happy to see you whenever you stop to get books."

They said their goodbyes, Paul seizing the moment, gave her a hug. He left knowing that her heart was probably crushed. His heart, too, felt very empty, a sore wound without a healing agent.

On Sunday, Paul preached on Matthew chapter 5, starting with the 43rd verse. He admonished his flock to not only love their friends and neighbors but to love their enemies as well. It was a good sermon and directed at no one person in particular. As he greeted his parishioners at the back of the church, he was surprised to see Maxine with a young man in tow. She introduced him as "Happy" Swenson.

"I'm very pleased to meet you," Paul enthusiastically voiced. And he was very pleased to see Maxine hanging onto someone else. Maxine explained that Happy belonged to Our Saviors Lutheran Church in town. The church was of a different origin than St. Peters. The two churches did not mingle.

He talked with them briefly, inviting Happy to visit again. The couple left.

Not wanting to eliminate time that he could spend with Rose, Joe had gone to his own church first, then went and picked up Rose and the two attended St. Peter's. Paul greeted them warmly.

Joe explained to Paul that he had already attended his church, then said, "I guess that I'll have enough "God sense" for all week."

Paul laughed and responded with, "Well, it wouldn't hurt any of us to attend church more than once in a day's time."

The church emptied and Paul walked to his home a bit melancholy. He soon perked up as he knew that he was planning a trip to St. Paul this week.

On Monday evening, putting all else aside, Mary, Joe's sister, was planning a bridal shower for Rose. Her mother, Lois, was helping her.

The guest list was quite large and no one had a home that would accommodate that many people.

"Maybe we should rent the Legion Hall?" Lois suggested.

Just then Rose and Joe walked in. Having heard the issue Rose said, "Why don't you have it in the basement of our church?"

So it was decided.

Joe and Rose had other things to reveal to them. They had been shopping and had bought their wedding rings. She was showing off her diamond. Everyone ogled over her new appendage. Rose was delirious with happiness.

They had also stopped at a second hand store to look over their wares. An oak dinning room table with six chairs held their interest. The table was void of extra leaves. At one time there had been an additional leaf but the second hand store owner didn't know what had happened to it. Joe remarked that this wasn't a problem, he could fix that. A couple of stuffed chairs for the living room looked appealing as well. Talking it over, Joe suggested, "They would be good starter items. We can always get newer things as time goes on. Mom is giving us the bed and dresser that I'm using at home."

"That will come in handy for company. Mom and Dad gave me a bedroom set for graduation. We can use it in the master bedroom," Rose added.

They made an offer on the items. The offer was accepted and Joe said that he would be by Saturday to pick up their purchases.

With little time left before the wedding, their planning went on.

Chapter Fourteen

Hutchinson Bridal Shoppe proudly showed off its wares. Laura, Rose and Joe's sister, Mary, were looking over their selection. The war just over with, material had not yet replenished itself. Even so, there were some to choose from. Besides selling wedding gowns and accessories, this store also sold other merchandise.

Shopping with her mother and best friend, Mary, Rose was enjoying the day. It being necessary that she capture some time to shop for her wedding, her employer had graciously given her the day off.

Not wanting to spend a lot of money on her wedding, Rose decided on a white formal with cap sleeves instead of a wedding gown. It was by far, much cheaper. A pair of fingerless long white gloves would add to the gown. Her choice of veil was made up of white chenille, white roses constructed out of glazed paper. Artificial pearls surrounded the roses, and of course, white netting over all. Finding a red dress that fit Mary to a T, was a bonus. A subdued red dress, that looked like strawberries and cream whipped together, was available in the size she needed for the bridesmaid. The two colors blended perfectly.

Laura found a cream colored suit that was on sale. A dashing red hat with red gloves, set off her ensemble.

Elated with their findings, the three-some left for home.

Wednesday morning the roads were relatively functional as Paul wended his way to Minneapolis. He would go there first, visiting the Lutheran publishing house for supplies. Snow banks formed the sides of the roads but traveling was not difficult. Material for Easter was foremost

in his mind. Yes, and looking up Tamar, too. He'd have to travel to St. Paul to see her. The Niedlichs, he was sure, would welcome the news about her welfare. He would call on them and assure them of her well-being after he returned home, although he was sure that they kept in touch with her via phone.

Proving to be a busy week for Paul, he had made several visitations the day before, checking to see how Luella and Lewis were doing and paying their neighbor, the Evans, a call, too.

His visit with Bernice and Bernard Evans went very well. Bernice imparted to Reverend Riech how impressed she was at the way he had handled the death of Luella's husband. Paul explained his love for Christ, saying that all good deeds done for mankind was likened unto doing them to Christ.

Luella thought, *I like this man. He's not boastful; it appears that he is filling Christ's granary instead of his own.*

Paul invited them to church and Bernard said that they just might do that.

He had also visited Otis and Marta Jenkins, along with their children, Bobby, Shirley and Benny. Marta was from Germany, having arrived in America with her parents when she was twelve years old. She had grown up on a farm ten miles South of Anderville. Otis and Marta were members of St. Peter's but were rarely seen in church. His visit with them went well, also. Paul hoped that he would see them in church oftener. Everyone needed a refreshing hour to replenish food for their souls each week.

Another visit took him to the home of John and Darlene Dieter. He had been told that John had been on the war front, was severely injured and had been sent home. They, as yet, had no children. It was inconceivable to Paul that after an experience of that magnitude, one would eliminate themselves from the house of the Lord. *People are different though, hopefully they aren't removing themselves from God's love,* was his thought. *I'm sure that I don't know all of the circumstances. For certain, I haven't walked in his shoes.* But he did have a good visit with them. John's back had been broken when he fell into a cavernous hole while in pursuit of German soldiers. He came back to the states wrapped in plaster of Paris. John and Darlene had married soon after his return to the states, even before he

was out of his body cast. His parents lived near by and were faithful members of St. Peter's. John was on the mend and soon would be able to work again. It had taken him a long time to recuperate.

Paul had a lot to think about on his travel to Minneapolis. He prayed for those that he had visited.

On this Wednesday, work was scarce at the lumber company and Joe had the day off. He drove out to their home-to-be, laying linoleum in the kitchen, linoleum which he and Rose had purchased on Monday evening. Tile flooring was in the bathroom, no linoleum needed there. Rose wanted a piece of carpet in the master bedroom. They decided to use throw rugs until they had built up enough funds to purchase it. They did buy a piece of carpeting for the living room. The floor in the guest bedroom would also wait until more money had been acquired.

Eager to help out at her home-to-be, Rose eagerly waited for Joe to pick her up at the end of her day's stint at the drug store. Grabbing sandwiches and drinks, they would hurry out to the country. Many a night saw the young couple still working at midnight. Joe's brother, James, along with his sisters, Mary and Margret, would often help, too. Much progress had been made toward their new home. Joe kept the snow shoveled from the sidewalks and driveway. That in itself was a big job.

Laura was sewing curtains for the young couple out of material that Rose had purchased. Light blue café type curtains with white rick-rack sewed at the hem line, would adorn her kitchen windows. With help from Joe's folks, the young couple had already painted the walls white in the kitchen, blue in the bedroom. The living room walls had been painted a cream color. Washing the walls down with Perfex, the couple felt that the walls would maintain another two years out of the existing paint.

Martin and Laura's neighbors, the Rice family, had given Joe and Rose a day bed that they had replaced with a couch. Happy to receive that gift, they had moved it to their home, placing it in the living room along with the two upholstered chairs they had bought at the second hand store. The green carpet, already on the floor, completed their living room furnishings. It didn't look too sparse for a first home, Rose reasoned. Wanting a new coverlet for the day bed, Rose decided to sew one from

drapery material. Her finesse in making things look cheerful, remarkably enhanced their dwelling.

Arriving at Minneapolis, Paul first stopped for lunch. Ordering a ham sandwich and a bowl of split pea soup, he read the paper as he waited. Bowing his head in prayer before he began to eat, he could then enjoy his food. He didn't tarry long.

Encountering great selections to browse through, the publishing house visit was relaxing for Paul. He picked out bulletins for Easter, some Easter music and also some Easter cards that he would send to his relatives and college friends, deciding to send one to Vivian too. After all, he hoped that they would remain friends. A book on the Gospel of John caught his eye and he purchased it also.

The publishing house purchases and lunch behind him, Paul set out for St. Paul where he hoped that he would meet up with Tamar. Stopping to get gas when he reached St. Paul, he phoned Tamar from there. Knowing the area where she lived quite well, it made for a speedier connect with her street.

Tamar was waiting for him in the living room. She greeted Paul with a big smile. Making eye contact with her, he smiled down at her as they shook hands. Introducing him to her landlady, Tamar then said, "Please have a seat, Reverend." Although she had been in his presence socially before, she was still a bit nervous.

"I'd like to take you out for supper, Tamar. Is that possible?"

"I have some lessons to do, but I can do them later."

Paul helped her with her coat and they left.

Conversation took over. Paul inquired about her studies. They were wrapped in a discussion of Bible History when Paul stopped at a nice looking restaurant. He opened the car door for her and gave her a hand in getting out. In a perfect gentleman fashion, he opened the restaurant door, and then aided her in removing her camel hair coat. She looked beautiful in a red jumper and white long sleeved rayon blouse with red saddle stitching on the collar. Her hair had been done in an upsweep which added to her years. Paul admired her lovely appearance, thinking that she looked like a school teacher already. He noted that since she had

started college her character blended more with the intellectual individuals, although she had always been able to hold an intellectual conversation before she had started college. *Maybe she has shed her high school image a bit more,* he mused. He was always looking for someone that he could converse with on a higher plateau.

"Rose is getting married and would like for you to be the organist. Maybe she has phoned you already," Paul volunteered.

"Really! I didn't know that she had a suitor."

"Because he's Catholic, it was kept quiet."

Tamar, wanting very much to be part of the wedding group, said, "I'll study late at night…If that's what it will take to be able to play for Rose's wedding."

"It will be a pleasure to have you with us again, Tamar."

"You know, Tootie actually could play for the wedding."

"Yes, she could. It would be nice to have you in our midst again, though."

Paul thought that he recognized a slight blush appear on her face as he spoke those words.

They went on discussing Rose's wedding, Tom's funeral—Tootie being the organist for that, and Tootie's over-all performance at the organ.

They never ran out of things to talk about, in fact time slipped away. Paul noticed, saying, "I best get you back to your studies. It will be late when I get home, too."

They said their goodbyes at the door, Tamar's heart sending a strong emotional message to her head that she could like this man. *What are his intentions?* she wondered. *Is he just being a good friend?*

"I'm to be the organist for my classmates wedding on Valentine's Day," Tamar revealed to her friend, Daniel Wheeler, as they were eating lunch in the cafeteria several days later. "I'm taking the bus to the music store after class to pick up some wedding music."

"I'd deem it a privilege if you'd allow me to drive you over."

Daniel was one of the "elite," so to speak, who had a car. Seeming that everyone who owned a car was one of the prominent citizens. Although

funds were scarce for him, he felt very blessed when his grandfather's car had been given to him.

Tamar accepted his offer.

After classes the two started out for the music store. Tamar felt very comfortable around Daniel. They had been in each others company quite often, usually eating lunch together. Funds being limited, he hadn't as yet, asked her for a proper date. Sometimes on Sunday afternoons, they would take long walks and discuss their lives, his as a farm lad, hers as a town dweller. Daniel lived on an Iowa farm, along with his parents, a brother and a sister, near a small town close to the Minnesota border.

Quite smitten with this young lady, Daniel however, having nothing to offer her at the moment, didn't allow his feelings to be apparent. Tamar, ultimately, did mention that her minister had stopped at her place of residence and had taken her out for supper. Nevertheless, she chose not to mention her thoughts on why he had singled her out.

The day for the bridal shower arrived. Things were flying into shape as Laura, Mary and Mary's mother, Lois, bustled about to prepare a lovely shower. The tables, in the basement of the church, were covered with white linen table clothes; red hearts, that had been cut from construction paper, were secured around the edges. The center piece of the serving table boasted a bouquet of red and white paper roses, made from tissue and crepe paper with red hearts made out of construction paper. From the bouquet to all four corners, twisted red and white crepe paper enhanced the table.

People arrived carrying their gifts.

Rose appeared with Mary, looking very lovely. She was wearing a red and white pullover sweater with a white pleated skirt. Her long blond hair, curled nicely, falling loosely around her shoulders, shimmered in the basement lighting.

Taking a head count, Ann, Joe's youngest sister, counted seventy-five people. The evening lent itself to visiting, guests all wanting to get to Rose to ask about the wedding and her plans for the future.

Dorthea, Amanda and Sophia were present. Dorthea's pregnancy was going well, revealing to her mother and sister that Dr. Meyers had an

intern working with him.

"He's very young, I'd say about twenty-five. He must have taken a few grades in the same year. Dr. Meyers has hopes of retiring soon."

"You don't say," Sophia responded. "I hope this new person knows what he's doing."

"I'm sure that he does, Ma," Amanda inserted, "They wouldn't have let him practice if the medical board didn't feel he was equipped for the job.

Other guests, also, were eager to hear about this new Doctor.

"What's his name?" asked Gloria, Maxine's mother.

"He has a German name, I believe its Keller."

"Yes, that is quite German, meaning cellar of course. Where's he from?"

"Now wait a minute ladies, I didn't ask any details," she voiced as she laughed.

"Surely there'll be a write-up in the paper about him. We'll have to check the next addition."

Opening gifts, Rose was elated with each and every gift. There were bed sheets, pillow cases, kitchen towels, mixing spoons, measuring cups, cooking pots and pans, a couple of blankets, several bath towels. Hearing that she could use table lamps and end tables, three families went together and bought her a nice end table for her living room. She was thrilled.

Standing at the door, Rose hugged and thanked each guest as they left. She was an abundance of cheerfulness, her exuberance overflowing.

Rose, Laura, Lois and Mary aimed their steps toward packing things together and wrapping up the evening.

"Mother Caridin, there's just too much here for us to pack out to our cars. I'll phone Joe to come and help," Rose suggested.

"That's a good idea," she replied, "Have him bring James along, too."

Margret and Ann were also helping to get things in order.

Finally, in her own room and ready for bed, Rose sent a prayer of thanks to her Heavenly Father for all the wonderful gifts and wonderful people. They would surely be able to take up housekeeping now.

The next evening, Joe picked up Rose and wended the car toward their country home. Both young people were ecstatic over the gifts that had so graciously been given them. Joe had pulled Rose close to him and seemed never to take his eyes from her. She kissed him on the cheek.

Once in the house, all of the shower gifts piled on the table and counters, they set to sorting things and putting them away.

The living room was kept free of items, like paint cans and such, in the event that visitors stopped by, which often happened. Neighbors stopped now and then, even offering their help. The daybed stood against a wall, the end table at one end of it, with the two upholstered chairs, one green and the other tan, standing at the opposite wall. For her confirmation, Rose's grandparents had given her a sixteen by twenty inch picture of Pilgrims bowing their heads in prayer. Joe had hung the picture over the daybed. It enhanced the living room and was also a prayerful reminder.

Rose standing on a step stool near the cupboards, Joe was handing pots, pans and mixing bowls to her as she put them in the cupboard. They finished putting things away. Pulling her to the living room, Joe seated her on the cot and sat down beside her.

Viewing their living room, Rose said, "It looks like a dream!"

"It's great!" Joe exclaimed, "And what's more, its our home!" He went on with, "Just a few more weeks and you'll be all mine." He hugged her.

"That will be different."

"You aren't going to abandon me now are you?"

"Certainly not! I've worked hard to keep us together."

"Yes you have. How can I be so lucky! You know what? Every night I say my prayers and thank God that He put the two of us together."

"What a pleasant thought! I'll pray the same thing."

"I don't have to work tomorrow so I'll bring my bedroom things over. We'll need something to sleep on after our wedding."

"What will you sleep on until then?"

"I could sleep here already but I think I'll crawl in with James."

"Well, the guest room is ready for your bedroom furniture and the master bedroom awaits my furniture."

The couple in no hurry to leave, their new home in good shape for the honeymoon night, basked in each other's company. A knock at their door

interrupted their chatting.

"Hello, Mike," Joe said as he answered the door. "Come on in."

"I saw that you had lights on and just wanted to stop to see if you needed anything."

Mike Shay was their landlord—for the time being anyway. They hadn't received any word on their loan as yet.

Joe offered him some coffee which he accepted, sitting down at the kitchen table. Rose and Joe were seated across from him. They visited for awhile.

Mike suddenly realized that he could probably get rid of one of his puppies, and stated, "Our dog just had puppies. Would you be interested in a puppy?"

"Oh yes, we need a dog," Rose promptly voiced.

"Come over in a couple of weeks and pick one out."

"We will," they both voiced at the same time.

Finishing his coffee he left and Rose and Joe finished tidying up and left for home.

Chapter Fifteen

Several Sundays had passed, Paul in his pulpit, was preaching on Matthew 18, with Peter asking Jesus, "Lord, how oft shall my brother trespass against me and I forgive him? Seven times?"

Jesus answered him, "I say not unto thee, until seven times, but until seventy times seven." Surveying his audience, he then continued with, "This lesson doesn't intend for you to get your score cards and pencils out. Jesus didn't mean for us to tally up the number of times that our brother grieved us. No, he wants us to forgive without reckoning how often we are called to forgive. Nor did he mean to forgive only our blood brothers. His implication here is for us to forgive anyone and everyone. God multiplies His pardons to us daily and he expects us do likewise." On went his delivery, congregators listening intently.

After church and in a reflective mood, Paul's thoughts traveled ahead to the end of February when life as a messenger of God, would pick up some paces. Ash Wednesday, proceeding in the Lenten Season, would soon be vying for his time. He would have to prepare two sermons each week. Asking God to uphold him during that busy time, he knew that he'd survive. Anyway, he loved that time of year.

On this Sunday, Paul made a mental note that John and Darlene Dieter were in church along with John's parents. Surely his visitations were bringing in the harvest. On the previous Sunday, Otis and Marta and their children had been in church. He'd stick with his visitations. Maxine was in church also, in the company of Happy. Appearing that this might be a steady situation, he was happy for her, and yes, for himself as well. *She must*

have given up the fight, he thought. The new doctor visited the church also. Paul had spent additional time talking with him, all the while Maxine had her eyes peeled on the doctor.

Timothy Keller, the new doctor, was tall and slender with a thick head of blond hair. He was quite good looking, too, carrying himself well. After Paul had concluded his talk with Timothy, Maxine had welcomed him in a regal fashion. *Poor Timothy,* Paul thought, *he'll be swamped by her possessive nature. Well, I can't be standing on judgment here, all I can do is pray for him, and yes, for Maxine, too.*

Parting with his thoughts, he went to fix himself some lunch. Gloria Schmit had again asked him to dinner and he had declined. He thought that he'd have to give in one of these days. Phillip was special to him and he reasoned that it would be a welcoming factor to be in his presence oftener than just at confirmation class. Anyway, he was to meet with the Abends for supper this evening. He looked forward to spending time with his good friends.

Again, missing Tamar's charisma at church, he thought, *well, soon the wedding day will be here and I'll be able to visit with her then. Patience is a virtue,* he admonished.

On Monday, seeing that he had finished all of his reading late Sunday evening, he decided to go to the library.

It was always a pleasure to encounter a visit with Vivian. However, his heart still didn't always obey his mental rule, but he quietly sent a prayerful thought to God for assistance.

He and Vivian talked about the upcoming wedding. Vivian knew the young couple. Actually, Joe was a member of St. Mary's where she, also, attended mass.

"That will be a first for me, first wedding to preside over," Paul voiced.

"You'll do fine," Vivian rendered, all the while thinking, *why couldn't things have worked out for us?*

They went on talking about the new doctor in town, material that they had been reading and other pertinent thoughts.

As Paul left, his heart pained him. He pulled himself together and went to the drug store, visiting with Rose for a brief moment. Her effervescent

personality would challenge anyone to get out of a melancholy mood. He enjoyed her exuberance. Buying some shaving supplies, he said his adios and left for home.

At college, Tamar studiously met each lesson with tough tenacity, working ahead as much as she was able in order to get a few days off. She would travel home on Wednesday after classes, the day before the wedding, so that she could practice with the bridal party that evening when the rehearsal would take place. Since her father's workday started early in the morning, his workday ended earlier in the day. He would drive to St. Paul to pick her up. Amanda didn't feel confident enough to maneuver a car in a city medium, as yet. However, she would enjoy the ride over with Herb.

Daniel and Tamar were enjoying another long walk on Sunday afternoon. This was getting to be quite a habit. They talked about Rose's wedding, St. Peter's church, Reverend Riech being single. That topic brought Daniel to a halt.

"You mean to tell me that he's not married?"

"No. He's just out of seminary."

Thinking about that for a moment he then said, "I think he's got his sights on you, Tamar."

"He's a very good friend but I don't think his intentions go any deeper than that."

"I wouldn't be so sure of that."

"I don't know. Since he's single, Mom has invited him for dinner a few times. The other ladies in the congregation invite him, too. I think that another gal, she graduated with me, has her sights set on him."

"Well, I'd be careful."

In his own sleeping area that night, Daniel thought about Tamar. He didn't want to see her slip away before his very eyes. *What should I do,* he questioned. *It will be a few more years before I'm out of college. Even then, I'll not be able to support a wife for a year or so. Can I honestly and sincerely ask her to wait that long?* Heart-sick and dejected, the dreadful thoughts kept flooding his mind. Finally, not able to come up with a just and fair solution, he said his

prayers and was able to fall asleep.

Tamar had gone to her residence fully rejuvenated from their talk and from the exercise the walk allowed. Looking forward to the wedding, she had been practicing the wedding music on an organ at the college. Still needing to pick up a gift for the couple she pondered on that, then thought about what Daniel had said concerning Reverend Riech. *Is he really interested in me?* she mused. *Would I make a good minister's wife? I really want to teach. That's my goal in life. I want to teach children how to get along in life, teaching them about Jesus above all.* Her thoughts were on Daniel and Reverend Riech as she dropped off to sleep.

On Saturday night there was another organized ice skating party. Having nothing better to do, Paul decided that he would stop by and watch the skaters for awhile. He bought himself a cup of hot cocoa and sat down on one of the benches. Maxine was there skating with Happy, but also skating with some of the other young men. He got a glimpse of the new doctor skating away, getting some good exercise. He noted Maxine sidling up to him. Soon the two were skating away. Listening for a time to the cacophony, the happy voices, the music, skate blades scraping across the ice, and an occasional "thump" as someone fell on the ice, he soon decided to return home and do some reading.

Just then one of the youth of St. Peter's skated up to him and said, "The ice is great, Reverend, come and join us."

"My skates are still in Milwaukee. I just came by to observe for a while."

"It's a fun gathering," he said as he skated away.

Maxine, true to form, was monopolizing Timothy's time. He finally grasped her game and decided to leave. Even then, Maxine was on him. "You're not leaving now are you?"

"I believe that I've had my share of exercise for today. I'll see you another time."

"But the party has just started."

Talk as she might, he stuck to his guns and left.

She was a bit frustrated but skated off to find a partner.

Happy, although he was a happy-go-lucky individual, also, was

thwarted by her actions. "My Wild Irish Rose" blared over the ice skating rink and Happy finally skated off looking for another partner.

The session drew to its close, everyone hurried off to their homes and vehicles, and Maxine stood holding the bag. *Where did Happy go?* she wondered. The lights went out and suddenly she knew that she had been dumped. With a five mile walk in front of her, she wasn't too happy. Sylvia, a class mate, had just removed her skates and asked if she needed a ride. A spark of luck for Maxine; she seized the ride. Sylvia happened to live close to Spruce Island and was going in her direction. Maxine's spirit had been crushed.

Out on the farm, Dorthea was planning ahead in hopes that she'd have all areas covered before the baby arrived. Her due date was in May. Gardening and baby chick time would soon be upon her. With the seed catalog in front of her, adjusting her growing body on the chair, she made out her seed order.

The brooder house needed to be cleaned and sterilized. The incubator had to be checked over. Work on the farm was plentiful. Amanda and Sophia helped her out occasionally.

Bill was getting harnesses fixed and machinery in tip-top shape. There never seemed to be a moment on a farm where there wasn't work looking one in the eye. Bill still tilled the land using horses. They had a tractor too, but with gas rationing the horses came in handy.

Amanda too, was perusing the seed catalog. Her intentions were to get the spring house cleaning done before Easter and then direct her attention to her garden. Then too, she and Tootie had their heads together organizing a baby shower for Dorthea. The plans for that was to be an after Easter affair. But it was never too early to make plans. Of course they both hoped that Dorthea would have a boy. It was almost a necessity to have a boy on the farm.

So went time spent in this Minnesota town.

Chapter Sixteen

February 14th, the day of the wedding, the morning sky unburdened itself of snow and more snow. Rose was beside herself with anxiousness.

"Rose," her father said at the breakfast table, "you'll be entirely wasted tonight if you don't calm down. Listen, a little snow is not going to ruin your wedding."

"You are right, Dad. I've said my prayers and now I'll leave the day in God's hands."

"I'd say that is the best idea."

Martin went off to teach school, the boys grabbed their books and set their feet toward school. Rose, along with her mother, hastened to prepare for a wedding. Art Simpson had given Rose the next couple of days off from work. There was work for Joe at the lumber company for this day and he adhered to it. He'd work anytime that there was anything that resembled work. No matter what. He had good reasons now to work and Rose was one of those reasons.

Mary and Lois were also busy getting things in rightful order. Mary had graduated with Rose and hadn't decided on a career plan for herself as yet. She did day jobs in the community, helping her mother whenever there wasn't anyone needing her help.

Pete and Lois had purchased a set of dishes for the couple. The box needed to be wrapped and being a rather large item, they planned on taking it to the church before the evening nuptials. They were also going to help decorate the church and help Laura and Rose with the preparations for the reception.

Rose's paternal grandparents had arrived from North Dakota on the

bus the evening before. They also, were in a helping mood. Things were flying.

Dorthea, wanting to go to the wedding, rushed around to get her morning chores completed. A crate of eggs, which needed to be transported to town, was looking Dorthea in the eye. She'd have to find time for that chore. Bundled up in her barnyard coat and gray scarf, carrying a pail of chicken feed, she slipped on a patch of ice. As she was falling she twisted herself to her side, hoping that landing on her hip would be less distressing to the baby she carried. Straightening herself out on the ground, a pain shot through her abdomen. Not wanting to give her body the added stress by pulling herself up, she knew that she needed Bill. In the barn doing his chores, her screams for help would be hard to hear. She called for him anyway. She needed help! He finally heard her distressed call.

Getting her to the house, he phoned to see if Amanda could come and help. It was snowing but driving carefully, Amanda pondered whether she'd be able to maneuver the car out to the farm. After all, she didn't consider herself a seasoned driver as yet.

"I'll drive you out, Mom," Tamar offered.

"You haven't driven on snowed roads that much either, Tamar."

"I have driven on some, Mom."

"Come along. We'll see what you can do."

Herb and Amanda had picked Tamar up after her classes ended the night before. They had arrived back home in plenty of time for Tamar to be at the rehearsal. As far as Tamar was concerned, she was ready for the evening affair. However, she would drive out to the church in the afternoon to run through the music one last time. *Practice makes perfect,* was her motto.

Arriving at the farm, Amanda, Tamar and Ruth, hastened to the house. Dorthea was lying on the couch.

"Just tell me why you had to do such a silly thing," Amanda kindly scolded.

"Well, I didn't deliberately try to fall. With the snow coming down it covered that patch of ice. I couldn't see it. Oh how I want to go to that

wedding tonight."

"How are the pains, still there?"

"They've stopped now. Tamar, will you go out and feed the chickens for me? The pail is probably where I fell. I imagine that some of the feed spilled out."

"I can do that. You just get yourself put together. Is there anything else you need to have done?"

"The separator and milk pails need to be washed."

"I'll do that," Amanda said. "Tamar can wash up your breakfast dishes and gather eggs for you."

"Maybe if I stay down for awhile I'll be able to go to the wedding."

Tamar and Amanda took over until Bill could come in from his daily chores to be with her.

Tamar, her overshoes on, coat wrapped tightly about her and a scarf tied beneath her chin, picked up her music and drove out to the church.

The janitors, Anna and John Lutz, were busy cleaning the church. They would be her audience. She chatted with them briefly.

Absorbed in her music, she didn't hear Paul enter the sanctuary. He stopped to talk with John and Anna a few minutes, then walked up to the organ.

"Are you ready for the big night?"

"As ready as I'll ever be. How about you?"

"With God's help I'll survive. It's my first nuptial officiation."

"I would imagine that while in seminary you were taught all the ministrations of your office."

"Yes I was. They prepared us well. I'm really not too concerned about this evening, although things can happen."

He thought a moment and then asked, "How is college life?"

"Great! I'm really enjoying it."

Since she hadn't been home on a weekend for quite some time, he asked, "Have you found a church to attend?"

"Yes, I go with the lady that I rent my room from."

He wanted to ask her about her off campus activities but with the janitors within earshot, he refrained. He wished her well and hurried off

to his study. *Maybe I'll get a chance to talk with her this evening,* was his departing thought on the matter.

After school, John and Eugene eating a snack in the kitchen, Amanda gave orders for them to shovel off Mrs. Oberling's sidewalks.

"Tell her that we'll pick her up at 6:00 to go to the wedding with us."

"Mom, I've got school work to do," John insisted.

"You will do that after you clear her sidewalks. Remember, anything that you do for her is like doing it for Jesus. Only what's done for Christ will last. Everything else will pass away."

The boys, although reluctant, took off on foot. The snow had stopped after it had sent two inches of its white "stuff" on the ground. Hastening their walk to Mrs. Oberling's, they hurriedly did the chores for her, returning home to do their lessons.

Tamar at the organ was playing, "Jesu, Joy Of Man's Desiring." The music for "The Bridal March" was at the ready. Casting her eyes to the mirror above the organ every few seconds, waiting for the bride and her father to appear in the rear of the church, she kept a flow of, "Jesu, Joy Of Man's Desiring," going. The groom; the best man, Joe's brother James; the groomsman, Rose's brother Samuel, were waiting close to the pulpit. Reverend Riech, book in hand, stood before the altar.

The bride appeared in Tamar's mirror. She switched her music and with great gusto struck the chord to, "The Bridal March." The congregation stood. Mary, Rose's maid of honor, carrying a bouquet of red and white carnations, waltzed down the aisle. The red dress was very becoming on her. Her dark hair, in a page boy style, sparkled. Mary's sister, Margret, the bridesmaid, looked equally as lovely. Rose, looking exceptionally beautiful, her hair curled about her veil, on the arm of her father, descended down the long aisle. Her radiant face manifested her happiness. She carried a white Bible, fashioned with different widths of white satin ribbon, and three white roses. The three roses representing the Trinity.

A few tears were shed as congregators witnessed the joining of these two individuals. Martin tried in vain to hold back tears. Wiping at his tears

with his thumb, he pulled himself together. Everything else went well and Paul pronounced them man and wife.

Arm in arm, they proudly walked to the back of the church, their faces punctuated with smiles. They were greeted by happy friends and kin, happy to see them "hitched."

After the wedding cake had been cut, the bouquet had already been thrown and caught by John and Anna Lutz's daughter, Mary Ann, which Maxine had tried desperately to catch, the young couple opened their gifts. Rose's employer and his family were present and they had given them a kitchen stool. Joe's two employers were also present with their families. They had given them an ironing board and an iron. A group of people went together and bought them two table lamps for their living room. Paul had given them a wooden cross. The intent was that when they experienced bleak days they had but to look to the cross and remember what Christ had done for them. Mrs. Oberling had given them a wall clock in the shape of a tea kettle, for their kitchen. Her parents had given them a radio, a mix master, coffee pot and toaster. Many other gifts, some of them in a monetary form, had been given them and they were graciously received.

Visiting with their relatives and friends, Rose hugged her grandparents, thanking them whole heartily for the gift of silverware. Mingling about, Rose thanked everyone for coming and for the gift that they gave. Joe, too, following behind, with great appreciation, spoke his thanks.

Pete, Joe's dad, invited some of their friends out to the family car where he offered drinks—not the kind that would appear in church. All the same, he was discreet about his spiked-up offerings, not wanting to embarrass the newlyweds, or Reverend Riech for that matter.

Dorthea, well rested, her normal flow of life retained, was immensely enjoying this joyous occasion.

Joe's brother and Rose's brothers were loading gifts into any vehicle that was available. Friends were offering their trunks and back seats of their automobiles to transport gifts to their new home.

Paul, hoping to get a chance to visit with Tamar, noticed that Maxine was chatting with her. He'd wait his chance, getting himself another cup

of punch as he bided his time.

He struck up a conversation with Laura as she stood near the serving table. Just then Maxine spotted him and walked over to greet him.

"Maybe we'll see you at the altar soon," she presumptuously said.

Laura was aghast at her boldness. Paul had her brazenness figured out months ago and did not flinch.

"Why, Maxine, I'm waiting to preside at yours."

"One never knows."

Turning to Laura he said, "The bride and groom are a fine young couple. I admire their godly approach to married life."

"We are thankful. She could have done much worse. We both like Joe."

He agreed and with that, excused himself and walked over to Tamar.

"You did great, Tamar. Your confidence was apparent."

"Only by God's grace. We do have a loving and kind Father."

"That bears repeating. You are home for the weekend I take it?"

"Yes I am. I'll play for Tootie on Sunday."

"Why don't you allow me to drive you home and we can talk about the hymns then."

Thinking about what Daniel had surmised about Paul, she still wasn't sure, but it did look like he was showing more interest than just a casual ride home.

"That will be fine. Our car was a bit crowded anyway. We brought Mrs. Oberling with us."

"Great. I have some work needing my attention in the office. I'll catch you in a few minutes."

Tamar went to tell her parents that she had a ride home, then went off to visit with her former employer and his family.

Chapter Seventeen

The morning after the wedding, Joe and Rose awakened, stars still lingering in their eyes, joyous of their togetherness, and still could not fathom that they were now one.

"Good morning, love," Joe said.

"And a good morning to you too, sweetheart." He put his arms around her and gently squeezed her. He was so in love.

"I'll get up and prod the furnace and get some heat in here," Joe dutifully offered.

Shivering in his boots, he made a trip to the bathroom first. He looked at himself in the mirror and thought, *What a lucky man I am! Dear God, keep me always mindful of that fact. Thank you for giving Rose to me.* His heart was so absorbed in this union that he was about to burst with happiness.

Rose blithely jumped out of bed, donned her robe and slippers, washed up in the bathroom, and went to prepare breakfast. She hummed a catchy tune.

There were still boxes setting around on the kitchen floor that needed to be put away. The two had put some things in order before they retired the night before. Rose had placed the table lamps in their respective places, with the exception of the one that was setting on top of the box that their dishes had arrived in. With some of their money they would buy another end table. Joe felt that he could make one. Now that he was working at the lumber company he supposed that he'd be able to use their tools until he had accumulated enough money to buy his own. He would ask them.

Returning upstairs, Joe put his arms around Rose and said, "Let's

celebrate with lunch in town today. Samuel Schwartz said that I could use his pickup to haul your bedroom furniture over here. Today might be a good day to do that. What'd you think? Monday we both need to get back to work." He kissed her cheek. She was agreeable.

After a leisure breakfast of juice, bacon, scrambled eggs, toast and coffee they both did the dishes. Setting about to put things straight, they worked at organizing the kitchen, getting rid of paper and boxes. Happiness prevailed and small talk wasn't necessary. They were wrapped in a cocoon of love. The sun shone through the windows bidding them a very cheery, "Good morning."

Tamar, in her four poster bed, stirred. *What happened last night?* she mused.

Step by step she went over every single detail. Paul had finished his desk work and had gone in search of Tamar. She was at the organ playing through the liturgy for Sunday's service. He had his coat on and helped Tamar on with hers. A few people were still milling about the church, cleaning up after the wedding. The bridal couple had already left.

Paul, holding Tamar by her arm so she wouldn't fall, walked her to his car.

Opening the car door for her, she gracefully seated herself. Guiding the car toward town he suggested, "It's still early. We could stop for a banana split."

"That's okay with me."

The café was open and quiet; just a couple of men sitting at the counter talking to the proprietor.

They sat in a booth.

Paul had prompted their conversation as they traveled the short distance to town, mostly about the wedding. He sallied forth again with, "What outside activities are you engaged in at college?"

"I'm in the chorus, but I wouldn't call that an outside activity."

"Isn't there anything that you do away from college, like bowling?"

"I have gone bowling before; I'd probably go again although it's not my cup of tea. On Sunday afternoons I usually take long walks. I like to walk. In the summer I enjoy going out in the woods looking for mushrooms and

wild asparagus. I read a lot too. I'm reading some of Zane Grey's writings now." She knew that this was not the time to bring up Daniel. Anyway, she had no idea what was on Daniel's mind, or Paul's either.

Well, Paul liked the sound of that. Maybe she hadn't been bombarded with suitors yet. *I wonder why,* he thought, *she's very, very attractive, intelligent and talented too. Maybe it's because she doesn't blow her own horn.* He finally asked, "Zane Grey—he's a western writer isn't he?"

"He's more of a mountain man and a man of the forest. What I'm reading right now is Betty Zane. It's about his grandmother. The story is filled with Indian activity. I enjoy reading about early life in America."

"A woman after my own heart! I, too, like reading about the Indians, their war upheavals and other doings. My great grandfather was married to an Indian maiden."

"Is that a fact? So you are part Indian."

Not having entered into a discussion of his background with Vivian, he was totally relaxed doing so with Tamar. Going on with casual talk, time easily slipped away. They left for Tamar's home. He parked the car along the side of the street, and talked some more. Finally he worked up enough courage to ask, "Would you consider a walk with me in the park, this Sunday afternoon?"

"I love to walk. There is probably a lot of snow around the park. It would have to be early since I have to get back to St. Paul."

"I've driven past the park and the children have some of the snow packed down for sledding. It's snowed since then but not enough to cause us a problem. Why don't we do this: I'll take you out to dinner, we'll take a leisure walk and then I'll take you to St. Paul."

Tamar wasn't sure that she should accept his offer of taking her to St. Paul. After all, it wasn't his responsibility to get her back to college.

"I'd love the dinner and the walk but my parents can take me back to St. Paul."

"I really don't get much uninterrupted time to talk with you, Tamar. I'd consider it a privilege to take you back to St. Paul."

"In that case I accept and thank you for the generous offer."

He pulled the car into the drive and walked her to the door, saying his "Good night."

Tamar rolled over in her bed, breathed a sigh and thought, *I wish he'd tell me what he has on his mind. Maybe he doesn't even know. For that matter, I don't even know what Daniel has on his mind. Now, what do I want? Do I want Paul to fall madly in love with me? Big question. Do I want Daniel to be madly in love with me? Another big question. Since I have been in Daniel's company the most, I feel very comfortable with him. Do I have what it takes to be a minister's wife—if that is what Paul has in mind?* Talking to herself, she had taken to calling Paul by his given name rather than, Reverend—not when she was in his presence, however. *Oh well, maybe the love bug will bite me soon and then I'll have my answer.*

She said her prayers and got out of bed and dressed, eager to help her mother.

Saturday evening there was another ice skating party. All week Maxine hadn't heard from Happy. With a forbidding temperament she threw Happy to the winds. She'd go to the ice skating party without him. After all, he'd left her stranded the Saturday night before. She'd show him who was boss.

Joe and Rose had invited Tamar to go with them. She had accepted. Tamar talking to her mother, suggested having the newly weds for Saturday supper. Trying to cajole her to her way of thinking, she said, "It doesn't have to be a big elaborate meal, just our usual Saturday night fare. They probably aren't set up for day to day housekeeping yet." She didn't have to convince Amanda. She was open to most of Tamar's ideas. Beside that, she liked Rose. She didn't know much about Joe; having him for supper would open an avenue in getting acquainted with him.

"It would be a nice Christian gesture Tamar. Maybe we should invite Reverend, too."

"If you want to."

Amanda tried phoning Paul. He didn't answered. She called his house. He didn't answer there either. Trying several times that day to get in touch with him, she finally gave up. It was getting late and preparations needed to be made for the supper.

Amanda's menu consisted of meatballs with noodles—which was an old German dish, homemade cottage cheese with chives, Jell-O salad,

peas from her garden which she had canned, and she reckoned that some of her pickled relish would blend well. Lemon pie, that she had baked that morning, would top off the meal.

Tamar had gotten in touch with the young couple and they would soon be at their doorstep.

Trying again to reach Reverend Riech, there was still no answer.

Joe and Rose, happy as larks, arrived at the Niedlich home. Tamar took them into the living room where they could visit. Phoning the Reverend one last time, Amanda was again met with silence on the other end.

Tootie helped her mother get things on the table. Soon the guests and family were called to the evening board. Herb said the prayer beseeching God to bless the newlyweds, also.

They graciously thanked him for his prayer.

Table talk centered around the young couple, many questions were brought up. Yes, they loved their country home. Yes, Rose was still going to work. Yes, Joe liked his work, but wished that there was more of it.

"I'm thankful for every minute I get to work, though," Joe announced.

Herb was very impressed with this young man. He didn't seem to shirk away from responsibility.

"They'll treat you right, Joe. I'm sure that soon you'll have full time work," Herb predicted.

So went their conversing.

Supper over with and dishes done, it was still a bit early to go skating. The boys took the couple out to see the rabbits. Herb tagged along. Joe and Rose, each holding a rabbit, marveled over their soft, luscious fur.

"If you'd like to start raising rabbits, we'll give you a doe that's going to have little ones," Herb offered. "They're good eating and some of the hospitals buy the meat. You can sell their hides, too."

Eager to make extra money, Joe accepted his offer.

Herb promised that he would bring a doe over as soon as one was ready.

The three-some took off for the skating rink. Music was blaring and skaters were laughing and enjoying the event.

Getting their skates on, the three joined in the fun. Skating away,

Tamar was surprised when a young man that she didn't recognize, came up behind her and waltzed her on down the rink.

Realizing his mistake he said, "Sorry. I thought that you were someone else."

"It's an honest mistake; what with everyone bundled up to keep warm. Faces are hard to recognize."

He skated Rose to a bench, then was off in pursuit of whoever it was that he was looking for.

Darwin, a classmate of both Rose and Tamar, asked Tamar for a skate. They whirled away, enlightening each other with their lives since high school days.

Soon Tamar caught sight of Paul sitting on the sidelines. She skated over and said, "You're not skating?"

"I just stopped to watch for a few minutes. My skates are still in Milwaukee. You're a skater I see."

"I like to skate. I think that everyone in this cold region skates."

She sat down beside him and said, "Mom tried to phone you. She wanted to invite you for supper. Rose and Joe had invited me to go skating with them so I talked Mom into having them for supper. She thought maybe you'd like a home cooked meal, too."

"I'm sorry I missed her call. I've been at the hospital. The new doctor had a patient that was dying and wanted a minister to pray over him."

"Oh dear. Someone that didn't know about God's blessings?"

"He was older, and yes, he hadn't given much thought about his salvation."

"I hope that he accepted Christ?"

"Indeed he did. That was a joyous witnessing. Sometimes, though, it goes the other way."

"I didn't know that we had a new doctor in town."

"Yes we do. He's been here for several weeks now."

They talked on and Paul asked if she wanted a ride home.

"I came with Joe and Rose. I'll probably skate for awhile and go home with them. I'll see you tomorrow," she said as she skated away. Paul left.

Happy was at the ice skating rink with a new found friend, Sally. She hailed from Galena, a town south of Anderville. He encountered a

meeting with her when he stopped to help her with a flat tire earlier in the week. Later he saw her at the café in Anderville and stopped to chat with her again. He asked her about skating. Her eyes shone when he mentioned it. Noticing her anticipation for the sport, he had invited her.

With a neck stretched out of proportion, eyes popped out of balance, and with a heart-sinking feeling, Maxine noted Happy's involvement with a new girl. She realized too late that she really did have feelings for him. Well, she wasn't about to cry in her milk, she'd look for that new doctor. Skating away, looking the entire rink over carefully, she was disappointed when he wasn't amongst them. Looking for other available skaters, she was again met with another disappointment—no unattached skaters were available.

As other skaters paired off, getting ready to go to the café for treats, Maxine was still not linked to anyone. *Oh well,* she thought, *I'll go with the group anyway. Maybe there will be a single at the café.*

The café echoed the pleasures of its merry, robust skaters, all participating in its mirth. Joe found a booth for the two ladies and himself. Mary Ann, the gal that had caught Rose's bouquet, ask if she could sit with them. Wholesome conversation took precedence. Happy, who was seated in an adjacent booth with his new friend, Sally, introduced her to Joe and his company. The two booths struck up a discourse about Joe's employment, Happy's employment with the cement plant, and of course about Sally and the town that she resided in. They were getting well acquainted and noted that she was a very pleasing person.

Maxine, unable to find a single man that was unattached, became disgruntled and left for home.

Arriving home around 11:00 that evening, Tamar had just missed her grandparents and the Becks who had paid their usual Saturday night visit to the Niedlichs. Tootie had supplied them with organ music for the evening.

Getting ready for bed, Tamar kept sneezing. "Wow, I hope that I'm not coming down with anything," she pronounced to Tootie.

"You could be...out in that cold weather all night."

"I know that it was cold. It was sure fun though."

Sometime during the night, Tamar had awakened with sneezes and coughing. She was running a temperature as well. A glass of hot water with some lemon juice and honey added, might knock the assailant off the track. Fixing that mixture for herself, she drank it, than crawled back in bed, covering herself with an extra quilt.

In the morning she had a temperature of 102 degrees. Tootie went downstairs to report it to her parents.

Upstairs, sitting on the edge of Tamar's bed, Amanda checked Tamar's forehead for fever. "You're not feeling good?" she questioned.

"I'll not be able to play this morning, Mom. I hope Tootie can do it."

"Don't worry about that. You just rest."

"I was suppose to go to dinner with Reverend Riech today. I'll have to call him."

"Reverend Riech? When did all of this happen?"

"I think he's just being friendly. You know, we've had him for dinner a lot. He's probably just returning the favor."

"I wonder. Well you get some rest."

"I'm going to phone Reverend Riech first."

Tamar went downstairs and phoned Paul. He was eating his breakfast.

"I'm sorry you're not feeling well. Of course I'm disappointed too. Be sure and take care of yourself. I'll check in later to see how you are."

With that taken care of Tamar took to her bed again. The rest of the family ate breakfast, got ready for church and left. Tamar fell back into a troubled sleep.

Saturday night, after Joe and Rose returned to their home, they decided that they would attend both churches on Sunday morning. Rose would go with Joe to St. Mary's and, likewise, he would go with her. However, Rose would not be able to partake of communion at St. Mary's, and moreover, Joe could not participate in the Holy Elements at St. Peter's either. This did not offend either one of them. They were just happy to be together.

Rose, so in love with her spouse, wanted to hold his hand while they listened to Father Dugan's sermon. She stealthily sought Joe's hand, covering their hands in the folds of her skirt, squeezed it with affection.

He looked at her, smiled thoughtfully and winked. He was one happy man, enveloped in the love of a woman that God had very graciously given him. He said a silent prayer of thanks for her. Rose, in the same state, couldn't believe her good fortune. Here was a man that truly loved her. What more could she ask for.

At St. Peter's, Tootie managed the organ very well. She had picked out simple pieces for the prelude, offertory and postlude. Her fingers deftly flew over the keys.

Timothy Keller was in church, seated near the back. He intently pondered Paul's words. He knew that there was but a breath between life and death and knowing that, he needed to prepare himself and his patients as well. So he listened.

Maxine was seated near the front with the rest of her family. She hadn't seen Timothy come in.

Having pronounced the benediction, Paul walked to the back of the church, singing the Three-Fold Amen along with the congregation.

The Schmits were one of the first to greet Paul. Gloria again invited Paul to take dinner with them. Since his plans had changed now that Tamar was ill, he hadn't planned anything for himself for dinner. He accepted.

Maxine at that moment saw Timothy leaving the church. Wanting to talk to him, she quickly shook Paul's hand and hurried from the church, trying to catch up to him. It almost worked. But she slipped on a patch of ice and fell. As she gathered herself together he drove out of the church yard. Shame and agitation marked her face. She walked to the family car.

That afternoon Tamar's temperature escalated. Amanda kept forcing ice cream down her and applying cold cloths to her body in hopes of reducing her fever. Tamar, uncomplaining, was however very uncomfortable. Her entire body ached.

At the Schmit dining table, Maxine held most of the conversation, telling Paul that she would be through school soon. Other factors entered into her chit-chat as well. Craftily she spun her ideas on the ability she felt she had to preside over a home of her own, good looks which she

assumed a man would deem a bonus in a wife, and anything that would direct one's thoughts to her.

Paul would kindly alter the discourse toward Phillip and Geraldine. No sooner had they finished a sentence and Maxine was digging in with prattle about some insignificant thing. Fred, Maxine's father, came to Paul's rescue now and again. There were other things to talk about. Necessary issues about the church. Fred was one of the council members.

After dinner and with a respectful amount of time having elapsed, Paul saw his way clear to leave. He had it in his mind to phone and see how Tamar was doing. Gloria walked out with him, wanting to warm up their car so that she could take Maxine back to Mankato. Paul got in his car and started it, letting it idle to warm up the engine. He got out so that he could scrape his windows. Noticing that Gloria was having trouble starting their car he went to assist her. Trying every conceivable action to get it started, it resisted. Paul finally offered to take Maxine for them.

"That's ever so nice of you, Reverend," Gloria said.

"I'm glad to do it, for you." Paul also knew that when doing things for others it was the same as doing them for Christ.

On the road, the car headed toward Mankato, Maxine unabashedly slid over in the seat, comfortably seating herself next to Paul. Paul, pulling over to the side of the road, turning to look at her, said, "Maxine, if a situation came up where I needed to gear down, it would be too difficult for me to do with you so close to the gear shift. Furthermore, I'm very sorry, but I have no interest in pursuing a relationship. My life is appropriated to Christ and I have every intention of doing His will. If I should ever consider dating, it would have to be with someone that has the same interest in the work that I have with Christ. Now, if you would please move over, I'll be happy to take you the rest of the way to Mankato." Maxine, feathers ruffled, pasted a scowl on her face which she didn't remove all the way to Mankato. Paul tried some conversation which wasn't working so he whistled away at a few simple tunes.

Chapter Eighteen

"Hello, Dr. Keller. This is Amanda Niedlich."

"Yes, Mrs. Niedlich. How can I help you.?"

"Our oldest daughter has a temperature of 103 and it's been climbing. We haven't been able to bring it down. Honestly, I'm very worried," she anxiously reported to him.

"With a temperature of that degree she needs to be transferred to the hospital. Could you do that?"

"Yes, we'll get her there right away. You will check her today yet, won't you?"

"Don't worry, Mrs. Niedlich, of course I'll look in on her today."

Hurriedly getting Tamar ready, Herb went to start the car so that it would warm up a bit. Instructions were given to the other children that Tootie was in charge and that they must mind her.

Helping Tamar to the car, she barely knew what was happening to her. She was on the doorstep of deliriousness, moving in and out of consciousness. Getting her situated in the back seat, Amanda held Tamar's head in her lap. Herb accelerated the motor to just above the speed limit, prodding the car along.

An orderly brought a wheelchair for Tamar and whisked her away to a nice cheery room. Doctor Keller's orders took over.

Paul, on his way home, thought about his day. He wasn't too pleased that he had to put Maxine in her place. Yet, he had to be honest with her and he was relieved that he had done that. It was just another of life's trifling problems and it would soon lose its strength as other issues moved

into its place. He was motivated to get home and see how Tamar was doing. Her image crossed his mind quite frequently. Would she be willing to accept the challenge of a life with him? Maybe she'd think him too old for a mate. Well, he'd soon find out, he hoped. In the mean time he would continue his request before the Lord. Striking up a great friendship with the new doctor, he thought about him for awhile. He didn't have a chance to talk with him that morning. Timothy seemed to be in a big hurry to leave church. Maybe he had an urgent meeting at the hospital. One couldn't begin to realize the emergencies a doctor had to face. Onward he went toward Anderville thinking about these thoughts, and giving some thought, too, to his own life in Anderville.

The newlyweds had been invited to Joe's folks for dinner. It was always a pleasure to gather around the Caridin's dining room table. Discussions were plentiful and most of the time, humorous.

Rose's bedroom furniture had been transported to their new place on Friday. Their home was now very livable and comfortable. The couple had bought a second hand Maytag washing machine on Saturday that a friend of the Caridins had for sale. It had belonged to an older couple. Joe had also bought some lumber to make a rabbit pen. Along with this he purchased a notebook to enter in cost of all material, lumber, feed etc.

He wanted to keep accurate records to enable them to see if there was any money in raising rabbits.

Arriving in Anderville, Paul went to the Niedlich home. John answered his knock and bid him to enter. Asking about Tamar, Tootie explained that she had been taken to the hospital and that he could see her there. He wasted no time in leaving the Niedlich premises. Tamar was apparently in more distress than he had thought.

At the hospital, Doctor Keller approached Tamar, checking her chest as he asked Amanda and Herb if she was allergic to penicillin.

"She rarely gets sick. There has never been a need to give her penicillin," Amanda answered.

He gave orders to the nurse about her medication.

Taking hold of Tamar's hand he said, "We'll get you up and running in

no time at all."

Her parents were happy to hear that.

"I'll walk you two to the door," he said to Herb and Amanda.

Once outside of her door they talked in low tones.

"I'm not sure if she has influenza. But that might be the case."

Herb, digesting that statement for a moment, then asked, "If not influenza, what else could it be?"

"I don't mean to cause you alarm but we could be looking at Poliomyelitis."

"Oh no," Amanda said, just above a whisper.

"Tonight should give us a clue. If her temperature goes down we've been visited by an angel. If it continues on a higher scale we could be looking at polio. Her temp just now was almost 104. I've ordered some penicillin for her. We'll watch her very closely for the next few days. Don't worry, she'll be well taken care of." Realizing that he had seen them at church that morning, he also offered, " I'll say a prayer for her too."

With that said he left to check on other patients.

Amanda went in search of a phone to call home while Herb went back into Tamar's room.

Tamar was out of it. Herb watched as the blanket rose and dropped with every breath. Paul stepped into her room. In low tones Herb and Paul greeted one another.

Herb related to Paul what the doctor had said.

"We'll storm the door of heaven begging God to restore her to health." Immediately Paul took hold of Tamar's hand and bowed his head. Herb took hold of her other hand. Words came from Paul with such urgency that Herb was certain that Satan high-tailed it to other corners. Surely God himself stood beside Tamar.

Quietly talking, the Reverend expressed his words of encouragement to Herb. Amanda walking into Tamar's room, was greeted by Paul. They shared their concerns: Tamar's school studies falling behind, her health in general. Again Paul tried to restore some sense of comprehension to their being.

Paul offered to buy them a cup of coffee. They accepted and the three walked to the cafeteria. Their conversation revolved around polio and

school and church functions.

Meanwhile, Tootie had phoned Bill and Dorthea and her grandparents to tell them of Tamar's unfortunate circumstance.

Bill and Dorthea quickly drove to town, dropping Dorene off at Sophia and Carl's home. Their old model T tolerated a heavier foot on the gas pedal as they headed for the hospital.

Opening the door to her room, they saw that the nurse was working with her. She bid them entrance. Dorthea immediately went and took hold of Tamar's hand, bowed her head and prayed silently over her. Unaware of the activity around her, Tamar was still slipping in and out of consciousness.

Paul, Amanda and Herb returned to Tamar's room. Dorthea hugged Amanda. In muted voices they talked. Bill, Herb and Paul moved out into the hallway to discuss Tamar's well being. Dorthea and Amanda took turns holding her hand.

The nurse coming back in with a pitcher of water for Tamar, said, "She's so young. Don't worry, penicillin is a marvelous drug." She left.

Soon Paul returned. "I'll pray for her again and then I have to leave. I'll try to come back later." Again he poured out his heart at heaven's door, shattering the stillness. His enunciation was clearly heard by those in his presence as he evoked God to reverse Tamar's illness. Everyone stood in awe at his prayer.

After he left Dorthea said, "It almost makes you feel like you are standing on holy ground when he prays." Everyone agreed.

It was getting on to chore time, time for Bill and Dorthea to leave. With Tamar resting comfortably, Herb and Amanda, too, thought that they would leave, returning after supper.

Supper over with, the children taken care of, Amanda and Herb went back to the hospital. Hesitating outside of her door, they wondered how they would find her. Entering, it appeared that she was in a peaceful sleep. They didn't disturb her. *Actually,* Amanda thought, *rest is what she really needs.* The nurse informed them that her temperature had not spiked any, holding steady for the moment.

A shadow filled the doorway, Amanda looked up to see Paul coming

in. Following his shadow were Bill and Dorthea. They again spoke their greetings. Just above a whisper, Herb and Amanda intoned their knowledge of Tamar's condition. Waiting awhile to see if she would waken, they continued on with chit-chat about the weather, making favorable comments about the new doctor, seeing as how he hailed from Wisconsin, also. They took to confronting world issues, too. Tamar slept on. Paul prayed over Tamar again and then left. Herb and Amanda soon left to be with the rest of their family. They walked out with Bill and Dorthea.

John was playing his guitar when Amanda and Herb returned. He was getting pretty good at it. Herb got out his fiddle and the two, trying to drive the gloom away, had a musical session.

Paul went home, sat at his desk, reflecting on Tamar and her illness. Was God trying to tell him that Tamar was not for him? Agonizing momentarily, he then thought, but then what about the Apostle Paul? If St. Paul had felt that way about serving God he would have quit mid stream. He was always being cast into jail, had been in a shipwreck, bitten by snakes and more. No, this did not mean that God wanted him to forget about Tamar. He would intensify his prayers.

Sunday night breathed its last breath. Rising from the bowels of darkness the inhabitants of Anderville shook sleep from their eyes as they approached the beginning of a new day. Bending with the newness of the day they went about their varied duties.

The newlyweds were on their way to work. Amongst other things on their mind was the issue of only one car. That coupled with the fact that Rose didn't know how to drive yet, she had no choice but to go to work with Joe. His work started at 7:30 and Rose's began at 10:00. They had that problem solved. Rose would stay with her parents until her hour arrived.

Joe escorted her into the house. He greeted his in-laws.

"Would you like a cup of coffee?" Laura asked Joe.

"I might have time for a quick cup." Rose hurried to get it for him. Small talk carried on and then Laura said, "Tamar is in the hospital."

Surprise registered on her face as she stated, "We were just with her

Saturday night. How did you find out about that?"

"Reverend phoned here last night to talk with your Dad about ice fishing. He mentioned that he had been up to see Tamar. She was in and out of consciousness."

"Her dilemma sounds pretty serious."

"Well, its not anything to sit on one's haunches about."

"I'll pray for her today whenever there's a lull in my work."

"That's a good idea."

"I'll pray for her too," Joe voiced.

Joe thanked Laura for the coffee and got ready to leave. Rose walked him to the door. "I'll be at the drug store to pick you up at five," Joe said, and kissed her goodbye.

Doctor Keller entered Tamar's room and noticed a young lady more alert than she had been the night before. She was still carrying a temperature but it was down considerably.

"Well, aren't you the spry one this morning. You gave us a bit of a scare yesterday," Timothy verbalized as he took hold of her hand.

"I'm sorry to cause such commotion. I feel a lot better than I did yesterday. I'd like to go home."

"I'd really like you to stay for a couple more days. The nursing staff is great here and the food isn't bad," he said with a smile and gave a wink to the nurse.

Tamar smiled and said, "Maybe just one more day. I need to get back to college."

"I suggest that you forget about college for this week. Which college are you attending?"

"Concordia, in St. Paul."

"You don't say! I went there for a couple of years too. I've seen your parents in church the last couple of Sundays. You were probably tucked away in St. Paul somewhere."

They went on chatting while Timothy checked her lungs. He was quite impressed with this young lady.

Tamar, too, was surprised at this young, good looking doctor. More so, she felt secure in the knowledge that he was a Christian doctor.

Later on that morning Paul came and paid her a visit.

"My, look at you. You sure had us on our toes yesterday."

"I'm sorry that I caused everyone so much concern."

"Well, everything is well that ends well. Thanks be to God for an answered prayer! I'm just glad to see you feeling better." He took hold of her hand.

It was Paul's day off and they talked about that and Paul mentioned that he was going ice fishing on Saturday. "It's high time that I do that. The weather will soon break and we won't be able to get on the lakes. Lent starts Wednesday, too."

Letting go of her hand he sat down on the chair that was near by.

"That will take up more of your time," Tamar stated.

"It takes more time, but I like the Lenten season. It brings us to our knees as we walk to Calvery with our Lord."

"I like Lent too, especially when we arrive at Easter, the climax of Jesus' walk for our salvation."

"Yes, Easter is what our salvation is all about."

"I'm sorry that I ruined our plans for yesterday," Tamar apologized.

"You needn't apologize, Tamar. It's something that couldn't be helped. We'll try again. Maybe this Sunday if you're feeling better."

He prayed over her again and said that he would see her later. He took his leave.

Sophia was busy quilting away when Amanda phoned to see if she wanted to go along with her to visit Tamar. She gladly accepted. With Ruth in tow they hurried on to the hospital. Paul had just left. Word got around fast that Tamar was in the hospital and she had a few other visitors as well. The morning went by fast.

During his break, Joe phoned Rose inquiring about their evening. It was intentionally planned that they would have their supper in town, then go to see Tamar at the hospital.

After work, they picked out a get-well card and a pretty scarf for her. They hastened to the hospital after they had eaten. Her room was cheery and Tamar, although she was still coughing and holding a temperature,

seemed astonishingly alert. They were happy to see this outcome and voiced that to Tamar. Paul came while they were there. He greeted them, chatting with them about their respective jobs. Another high school friend of Tamar and Rose's walked in. Paul knew that he was outnumbered. He said a prayer over her and then left.

On the way home Rose quizzed, "I wonder why Reverend doesn't date Tamar. It seems to me that they would be a good match?"

"Maybe so. Might be he thinks that he's too busy for a wife," Joe answered.

"I wonder?"

Chapter Nineteen

Ash Wednesday Service was highly attended. The Niedlichs were amongst the worshipers, with the exception of Tamar. Dr. Keller had talked Tamar into staying at the hospital one more day.

Following the service Herb and Amanda made sure that they experienced a talk with Dr. Keller. He in turn, relayed to them that he was very pleased with Tamar's recovery.

"I'll release her tomorrow," he went on. "However, she needs bed rest for the rest of the week."

"That's easier said than done," Amanda replied. "I'll try and keep her down, though."

"Her lungs need the rest," he advisedly stated.

After talking with Timothy, who was the last to leave the church, Paul went to the hospital to see Tamar. He had been to see her every day, and sometimes even twice on the same day.

"You're looking very chipper, Tamar."

"I'm feeling very well. Thank you."

"I take it that school is out of the question for the rest of the week."

"It is. Dr. Keller really wants me to stay home another week, but I have to get back."

"Don't over tax yourself, Tamar."

"I won't. I'll rest a lot. I'll not start back to chorus for a couple more weeks."

They went on talking about the Ash Wednesday service and other pertinent things. Paul took hold of her hand and said, "Tamar, I'm very

happy that you broke through this illness."

Tamar, not really knowing what to make of his announcement, said, "I thank all of the people who prayed for me and above all, I thank God for His wonderful gift of life!"

"Indeed we should. Maybe, if it isn't too cold on Sunday, we can take a short walk in the park."

"That might be a possibility. Perhaps a bit too soon, though."

"Will you be coming home the next weekend?"

"I probably will."

"Maybe I can call you during the week and see how things are going."

"That would be fine."

Paul didn't force her to any commitments. Now wasn't really the time. He'd wait until she was feeling better.

Taking his leave he took hold of her hand and offered a prayer of thanksgiving, also asking God to watch over her. He smiled and said, "I'll drop by the house to see how you are doing. God bless and keep you."

"Thank you for all that you have done—all your prayers and concerns."

"It is a godly thing to do." He squeezed her hand and left.

The next morning Timothy went to Tamar's room and checked her lungs one more time. He sat down in the chair next to her and visited with her a short while. He approved in what he saw in this young lady. Then he said, "I'll see you in my office on Friday."

Smiling, with dimples obvious, she answered, "Okay, I'll be there."

Amanda went to get Tamar and her gifts and the bouquet of flowers which she had received from her uncles, Fritz and Walter and families.

Getting her situated at home, she wasn't ready to be stowed away in her bedroom.

"You can rest on the couch, Tamar," Amanda offered.

Picking up something to read for herself, she settled in.

The phone rang around three that afternoon. Amanda answered the call, which was for Tamar. She called Tamar to the phone.

"Who is it?" Tamar asked.

"It isn't a voice that I recognize. It's a man."

"Hello."

"Hi Tamar. I was worried about you. Haven't seen you in school."

"Hi Daniel. I've been in the hospital with the flu. Thanks for worrying about me."

"Are you okay?"

"I'm much better and will be back on Monday."

They went on talking about school activities and their usual Sunday afternoon walks. Daniel suggested driving over to see her.

"I'm doing fine now, Daniel. Save the gas money. I'll be back in a few days."

"I miss you."

"It sounds good to be missed. We'll catch up when I get back."

They brought their conversation to a close.

Joe and Rose went to visit Tamar at the Niedlich home that evening.

"You're looking good," Rose said.

"I'm feeling much better. Thanks."

"There's another skating party this Saturday night," Rose said with a mischievous gleam in her eye.

"It would be fun, but I had better forget about this one."

Joe spent time talking with Herb, telling him that he had the rabbit cage finished.

"Good! We can bring a doe over on Saturday."

Joe revealed to Herb his luck at obtaining a job working for a farmer. He would work for Stein Baker on the days that he wasn't working for the lumber company. Stein lived five miles north of them. Joe appeared very happy about this new challenge and Herb congratulated him.

Rose enthusiastically told of their new puppy, Tiger.

Joe said, "She's as excited as the little fellow is. He wags his tail, knocking over everything in his path. Rose hasn't done that yet." Everyone got a good laughed at that.

Soon a knock at the door manifested Reverend Riech's appearance. With the Caridins still present, stimulating conversation took hold. Everyone was having a great time visiting, albeit Paul wasn't getting much of a chance to have a private talk with Tamar. His thought: *That's probably out of the question now that she is home from the hospital. I'll patiently await my moment.*

With Tooties help, Amanda made coffee and placed cookies on several plates for their guests. No one wanted to leave, but guests knowing that Herb needed to be up early, relinquished the inspired conversation and took their leave. As Paul was leaving he took hold of Tamar's hand and said, "It's so good to see you feeling much better." They said their goodbyes.

Tamar felt that her visit with Doctor Keller on Friday was intriguing. He spent a lot of time talking with her, more than he professionally needed to, she thought. Then giving her a "clean bill of health," he said, "I hope that I will see you in another environment than the hospital next time, Tamar."

"God willing, you will. Maybe at church."

Gloria, somewhat puzzled by their car acting up as it had, phoned Maxine and suggested that she take the Greyhound Bus Line to get home on Friday after school. Maxine was a bit upset about that rock in her path but agreed.

Getting herself to the bus depot and acquiring a ticket, she purposefully ascended the steps into the bus. The bus driver, a good looking man, who appeared to be about twenty-six, was agape at the beauty of this young lady. She sat near the front. It was nearing his coffee break and he thought that he would take his break in Anderville. Upon entering the station at Anderville, he took Maxine's luggage from her, saying, "I'll carry that for you, Miss."

"Why, thank you."

She sat at the counter with him, and as he was eating they talked about various things. In the midst of all of this conversation she had given him her phone number. *Bus drivers can't be bad people,* was her thought. When he was ready to leave he said, "I'll probably see you again next Friday afternoon."

"I imagine so," she responded.

Saturday morning, Herb, Tamar, John and Eugene took the doe out to the Caridin home. Tamar was happy to see the Caridins little "nest", and

Rose enthusiastically showed her the entire house.

"You have it fixed so cute, Rose," Tamar voiced.

They talked on for a bit and as they were leaving, Rose said, "I'll miss you at the skating party tonight."

"I'd love to go but I better follow orders. You can tell me all about it next time I see you."

Martin, eager to go ice fishing, went to pick up Paul. As he drove up to the church he saw a man's leg hanging out of the office window. *What's this?* he asked himself. Then another leg appeared. Realizing that it was Paul, he wondered what happened.

"Are you okay?" Martin asked.

"I'm okay, just couldn't get the office door open."

"What a way to have to get away from your work," he said as he chuckled. "We had better take care of that door before we go ice fishing." So it was. They fixed the door first.

The day was made for ice fishing. They got to their destination eventually and enjoyed the rest of their day.

That night at the skating party, Maxine was in great form. She was thrilled that someone was interested in her and it showed in the way she flounced herself about. She "deviled" any man that came in her path.

Soon Timothy Keller arrived, skates were pulled on and skating was strongly pursued. He loved to skate; the wind in his face, scarf flying behind him, stocking cap pulled down over his forehead, exercise in progress. Maxine, noticing him, made a quick dash to his side. He coddled her for just one skate around the rink, he hoped. Noticing Paul sitting on a bench, he two stepping Maxine over to another available skater and went to join Paul. They winged their way into a deep discussion about philosophy, moving on to Anderville and its inhabitants. Opting for warmer surroundings, Timothy took off his skates and they left for the café. Over a hot cup of coffee and a hamburger, they continued on with their conversation.

Maxine looked the entire rink over for Timothy and there was no Timothy to be found. Reverend Riech was gone too. *Oh well, what do I care,*

she thought. *I've found an agreeable companion anyway.* Happy was there with his new friend. That didn't discourage her any either.

The skating party ended and Maxine took her skates and headed for home. Arriving at home her mother handed her a piece of paper and said that there had been a phone call for her. Maxine looked at the number and guessing that it was from Lawrence, hurried to the phone. Lawrence Johns was the bus driver she had a conversation with on Friday. They talked their way through thirty minutes. Gloria didn't wait up to talk with her, finding her bed more relaxing after a full days work.

Chapter Twenty

Through Paul's visitations in the Anderville area, he had often called on a family that from time to time visited St. Peter's. They were not members. Encouraging them, he hoped that they would heed his pleading, laying upon them the peace and blessings one received from God's word. The Ramier family consisted of Tom: the father, Evelyn: the mother and three children. Christa was the oldest at four years of age; Robert was two and the baby, Shirley, was three months old. This family lived in town, not far from the post office where Tom worked. Paul's visits had finally been successful and another family had been marked for the kingdom of God.

On this first Sunday after Ash Wednesday, the children had been slated for their baptism. It was a situation that the parents had failed to carry out during their former years. Tom and Evelyn had both been baptized as infants. This was Paul's first baptism.

The altar flowers had been purchased by the Ramier family for this day. All was in readiness. Paul, with his black robe fitted about him, stood in front of the altar. As he looked over his audience, colorful winter hats were nodding about. The children and their sponsors walked toward the altar, assembling themselves in front of Paul. Christa was old enough and understood what was happening, behaving very well. Little Robert, a mama's boy, cried, screamed and fussed until Evelyn had to go to the altar to quiet him down. He screamed when Paul applied water to his head. Paul kept his composure, going on with the service. After the Order of Baptism was over, Paul, although it was not a required mandate of the rigid order of baptism, took Robert from his mother and soothingly

talked to him. Handing him back to Evelyn, he continued with the service.

Tamar's heart did a flip-flop as she witnessed this exchange between the baptized one and his minister. *He's so wonderful with children,* she thought. Another action of Paul's which drew him a bit closer to Tamar's heart.

After the service people welcomed the Ramier family, enlightening them and taking time to chat.

As Tamar was leaving church, Paul shaking her hand, offered, "I'd be glad to take you home, Tamar, if you don't mind waiting?"

"No, I don't mind. I'll wait."

Timothy was in church also and Maxine noticing him, made a beeline for him, ascending upon him as the interchange between Tamar and Paul was developing.

Tamar moved toward the front of the church, seating herself in a pew and listened to Tootie as she brought the postlude to its finale. Timothy, having quickly concluded the conversation with Maxine, noticing Tamar engrossed in the music, walked over and sat down beside her.

"And how is my favorite patient this morning?" Timothy asked.

"Your professional finesse worked wonders, I'm feeling fine, thank you!"

"Well in that case I'd like to offer you lunch and conversation."

"I'd love to! Only I can't today."

"How about next Saturday. Can I pick you up at about six that evening?"

"I'd love that."

He stayed and talked to her for a few more minutes and then took his leave, shaking hands with Paul as he was leaving.

Maxine on the other hand, had noticed this status between doctor and patient and thought, *why is he buddying up to her, I'm better looking than she is? I'll never understand men!* She left in a huff.

Tamar thought about Timothy after he left. She was sure that this upcoming business with her doctor could be called a date. Her heart was excited for a moment. His good looks would make anyone's heart palpitate, at least for a second or two.

Paul had been busy greeting his congregation and failed to perceive this exchange between Timothy and Tamar.

"I'll be with you in a few minutes, Tamar," Paul said as he was on his way to his office to remove his vestment. Grabbing his winter coat and fitting himself into it, he walked over to Tamar saying, "Okay young lady, shall we go?"

Smiling at him, she voiced, "I'm ready."

On the way out of the church yard Paul suggested going to Spruce Island to eat lunch. Tamar was agreeable.

On the way they talked about the church service.

"I liked the way you quieted young Robert after his baptism," Tamar voiced.

"I didn't want him to have any bad feelings about his baptism, although he might never remember it."

"He might remember. In my psychology class I've learned that a child can remember very happy times and very sad times at a young age. Your soothing voice should quell any ill toward his baptism, though."

He looked at her and with a genuine smile said, "Thank you for that sentiment."

They talked on about personal likes and dislikes and found that they were impressively compatible.

Seated at the café, Paul again inquired about how she spent her time away from college.

"Well, as I said before, I do like to walk and read and that's about all that I accomplish in my spare time. I help my landlady a lot, too."

Paul liked what he heard. "You don't go ice skating in the city?"

"No. I'd rather do that in Anderville."

"How about if I pick you up at your home on Saturday for skating?"

Tamar, remembering that she was to go with Timothy on Saturday, said, "I can't this Saturday but we could go early Sunday afternoon."

"That would be great. I'll take you back to St. Paul afterwards."

"That would be most pleasurable."

They had discussed their earlier lives, his in Milwaukee, hers in South Dakota and Minnesota. Feeling that they knew one another a bit better, Tamar was appreciating the comfort she felt in his presence. He, like

Tamar, feeling very comfortable, thought that this young lady could make him a happy man.

On their way back to Anderville they started singing some tunes that had found their way across the ocean from Germany, like, "Auch Du Leiber Augustine," "Du Du Liebst Mir in Herzan," a beautiful love song. They slipped into some American songs, starting with, "In the Good Old Simmer Time." Singing their voices out they ended with a hymn that had been sung at church that morning.

"Tamar, you have a great voice, we should sing a duet at church one of these Sunday's."

"You have a great voice yourself." She wanted to call him Paul but he hadn't offered that phase to their relationship yet.

Driving into town he felt that she probably needed her rest so he drove to the Niedlich home. Walking her to the door, Tamar asked, "Won't you come in?"

"I'd love to do that for a few minutes."

He greeted the family as he entered. Bobby was visiting John, listening to his guitar renditions. Paul greeted him also and sat and talked with the two for a few minutes. After conversing with Herb and Amanda for awhile he excused himself and left for home, wanting to phone and talk to his mother to see about her well being.

Eager to push herself into her lessons again, Tamar felt at ease back at school. However, she was overwhelmed by all the learning that she had missed.

At lunch time Daniel joined her, very happy to see her back in the swing of school particulars. He voiced, "You look good, Tamar. I'm so glad to see you!"

"I'm very happy to be back. Now I need to get caught up. It will take some heavy concentration on my part to get me to where I should be."

"I'd be glad to help you, Tamar."

"Thanks, Daniel. I think that I'd move along faster if I went at it by myself."

They talked on and then Daniel asked, "Will you be staying in the city this weekend?"

"I'll have to see how my lessons go. If I stay I'll have to regiment myself to studies all weekend."

"That doesn't sound like much relaxation."

"I know. But I must get caught up. My main goal is to finish college and get out there and teach."

Daniel was a mite disappointed. He would not have his weekend walking partner. They talked on about other things. Daniel offered to walk her to her living quarters, but Tamar knew that by doing that it would take extra time, time which she could use to bring herself up to par.

Paul phoned Tamar on Wednesday night after the Lenten church service. She was busy with her studies.

"How are you doing?" he asked.

"You wouldn't believe all of this work I have to do to get back in line with the others."

"I'm sure that's true. Don't push yourself too hard."

"I'll try to get the rest I need, but if I'm not able to get this done before the weekend I'll have to stay here so that I can study."

"You are really driven to get this education aren't you?"

"It's very important to me."

He didn't keep her long and said that he would call again the next night. He was very eager to see her on the weekend.

The next day Paul needed to return some books to the library and pick out some to read. Being especially interested in the life of Luther he hoped that the library offered books about him. Then too, the life of George Washington was intriguing. Maybe the Lakota Sioux with their beautiful culture would be very interesting. He'd scan the bookshelves and see what he could entertain himself with.

Entering the library, Vivian was seated at the front desk. She smiled warmly as her eyes affixed on him. Paul smiled in return and felt that some of the emotions that he had carried were diminishing. Yet, he had some feelings that surfaced, striving to push them back, he spent a bit of time conversing with her.

Poring over the rows and rows of books he found one on Daniel Boone that appealed to his senses. Finding Betty Zane, by Zane Grey, he

decided to delve into some of his work. He'd see what fascinated Tamar about this writer. There were a few books on Anderville and he checked two of those out, plus a book on the last Sioux war.

"Looks like you are in for a lot of reading," Vivian remarked.

"I do like to read in the evenings. It sets my mind at rest."

Completing his mission he picked up his books and left.

That evening he phoned Tamar again. She had stayed up until midnight the night before to study and she felt that she had advanced in her studies enough to be able to go home for the weekend. Paul offered to go to St. Paul to pick her up on Friday afternoon. Expressing to him that she would be taking the Greyhound home on Saturday morning, she added, "I'm spending Friday evening at my studies."

"Please take care of yourself, Tamar. I care about what happens to you."

"Thank you for caring." Again she wanted to say, *Thank you for caring about me Paul,* but she hadn't been given the privilege of calling him by his given name as yet.

"I have placed my life in God's hands," she added.

"Your heart is in the right place, Tamar."

They finished their conversation and Tamar went to her books and proceeded with her make-up work.

Friday finally arrived and Maxine was in ecstasy. She had talked to Lawrence, and had even seen him during the week. His home base was in Mankato. His parents also lived in Mankato. Boarding the bus, Lawrence had saved the seat directly behind the driver for her. They whiled away the time chatting all the way to Anderville. Maxine was wanting him to come to Anderville on Saturday night for the skating party. Since his work came first, he had to decline.

"But I'll see you during the week on my days off. We'll go dancing one night."

She seemed a bit disappointed but agreed to his offer. Stopping the bus, Maxine was the only person getting off. He held her hand a moment, then stooped to kiss her. As the bus was leaving she waved, then walked

into the café to phone her mother.

Before noon on Saturday, Tamar rode into Anderville via Greyhound. She walked home. The wonderful aroma coming from the kitchen as she entered made her feel warm and secure at being home. Amanda was baking coffee cake. She hugged her mother and they immediately discussed her health.

"I'm really feeling very good, Mom." she informed her.

"After burning the midnight oil, trying to get your work caught up, you should spend today relaxing and resting. You don't want to get sick again. Remember what Dr. Keller ordered." her mother warned her.

Tamar, remembering that she was going out with Dr. Keller that evening, said, "Well, tonight when Dr. Keller picks me up you'll most likely get his opinion on my welfare."

"Dr. Keller? What ever happened to Reverend Riech?"

"Well, I'll be seeing him, too, on Sunday."

Amanda a bit shocked at her daughters excess, said, "Tamar, you can't be going around with both of these men at the same time. It's not proper!"

"Mom, I'm not sure where all of this is going. I'm not even sure what their feelings are about me. Maybe they are just being friendly. I'm not even sure that I have feelings for either one of them. But when I find out Mom, I'll discuss it with you, okay?"

Amanda, looking at Tamar, thought about the picture that she had just painted for her, then lowering her eyes to the dough in front of her, she sliced apples into it.

"Well, you best rest a bit now."

That evening at six, Timothy was at the Niedlich door. Amanda answered his knock.

"Good evening, Mrs. Niedlich. I hope that you will allow me to escort your daughter this evening?"

"Yes, of course. Do come in."

Eyeing Tamar, donned in a navy blue sweater and navy plaid skirt, standing in the kitchen doorway with her coat over her arm, he greeted her pleasantly with high expectations of spending an evening with her. He

then spent time chatting with Herb.

Tamar observed Timothy in his casual attire, very spiffy looking, and thought about this scene rolling before her. How was it that she, just a plain Jane, so she thought anyway, could be so rich as to be entertained by a doctor; and also a preacher! God was good, was her feeling. Timothy, with blond hair and brown eyes, was tall and handsome; not as tall or as handsome as Paul though.

Helping Tamar on with her coat, they left.

Opening the car door for her, she gracefully seated herself.

Once on the road he said, "I don't think that we should attempt ice skating tonight. Having you out in the elements for any length of time would not be wise. How about getting something to eat and seeing a movie?"

"I haven't seen a movie in ages. That suits me fine."

"Good!"

Surveying the road ahead of him, he then asked, "How are your classes coming?"

"I really had to cram to get them to where I could get away for the weekend."

"Well, I'm glad that you made it. What do you do for entertainment in the big city?"

Tamar, realizing that it was time to let both Paul and Timothy know that she had another admirer, said, "Saturdays I spend helping my landlady and getting ready for Sunday. Sunday afternoons I usually spend walking with a young man from college who wants to become a teacher."

"I can't blame anyone for pursuing you, Tamar. You're intelligent, nice looking and a very nice young lady, I might add."

"Thank you, Dr. Keller."

"We can dispense with this 'doctor' business Tamar. This is a social engagement. Please call me Tim or Timothy."

She conformed and they went on talking about other issues, Tamar asking him about his life in Anderville. As they were eating they talked on, never running out of words and topics. Tamar was quite taken with Timothy, and interested in his life as a youngster in Wisconsin. His heart had definitely been captivated, not that she proposed to do that.

Moving on to the theater, Timothy was a very fine escort. Tamar was feeling very much at ease.

The movie was a love story with Clark Gable. One of the scenes was very moving and Timothy took hold of her hand. She was a bit startled, hadn't thought that they had advanced to that point yet. *Maybe it's the movie that has enticed him to make that move,* she thought. Then, too, the thought was, *in his profession he'd have to be very compassionate and I'm sure that he is very affectionate.* She grew fascinated by her hand in his. His hand felt warm, soft and smooth. But then, being a doctor, she was sure that soft pliable hands were an important implement when dealing with woman and babies with their tender skin, or even for performing surgery, for that matter.

At the skating rink Maxine was having her fun. Looking around for Dr. Keller, she was disappointed that he wasn't around. Reverend Riech wasn't there either. She dismissed both men from her thoughts and skated toward a couple of young men that she hadn't seen at the skating parties before. They both obliged and both tried to out-do the other with their humor and attention for her. She bounced from one to the other.

The skating parties were a diversion for Paul from his weekly schedule. On this evening, though, he had decided to stay home and do some reading. Getting into another world through a book appealed to him, although his thoughts were not far from Tamar. He was eager to be with her the next day.

After the skating had ended the skaters again went to the café for refreshments. Maxine walked in the café with both of the men that she encountered at the rink. The scene at the café was the same as any other Saturday—noisy.

The feature at the theater had ended and Timothy suggested a hot fudge sundae. Tamar was in agreement. Entering the café they could see that it was rather crowded with the skaters. Maxine noticed them immediately. She became very sullen. The two young men couldn't understand what incited her changed personality. Finally, one of the men had his fill of her moodiness and decided to leave, thinking, *She's pretty but that's all she is.*

Maxine, pained by seeing Tamar and Timothy together, decided to

leave. Walking to them on her way out, in an inconsiderate tone, she said, "Well, well, what have we here."

"Hi, Maxine," Tamar answered, "How are you?"

"Well, I thought you were sick. You've got your doctor out with you to chase the flu bug away, I gather?"

Timothy, appalled at her attitude, said, "Maxine, I've invited Tamar for the evening. If we are bothering you we can go elsewhere." He got up, grabbed Tamar's coat, helping her on with it, and putting on his own, they left for a quieter place.

Maxine stood with hands on her hips, watching them leave and putting on her own wraps, she left for home.

Timothy drove to Spruce Island. Surely there would be something open there although it was near 10:30. They were in luck, a group of people had been celebrating a wedding anniversary in Spruce Island's only café, and were just getting ready to leave. They finally got their hot fudge sundae that they had left behind in Anderville.

Glancing at Tamar, he smiled and said, "Both of our names start with the letter T."

"They do for a fact. Beside that they are both biblical names."

"Is that right? I didn't know that Tamar was a person of biblical importance."

"I don't know how important she was but she does come to us out of the Bible."

"That's interesting. Your name is also German."

"It is. It means sweet, nice or cute," Tamar replied.

"How striking. That really describes your personality, too. Well, mine means cellar." Looking charmingly into her eyes, he continued with, "Imagine this: A nice, cute, sweet maiden descends to the cellar with her admiring fellow."

That produced some laughter after which Tamar said, "I hadn't thought about that. Well, your last name may mean cellar but you don't portray the cellar person at all! You're bright and cheerful."

"Thank you. I appreciate that."

They talked on and then being her physician he knew that she needed her rest so they left.

Arriving at the Niedlich home, turning off the car, Timothy put his arm around her shoulder and stated, "I like you very much, Tamar. Our time together has been very enjoyable. May I see you again tomorrow?"

"I can't tomorrow. I'll try and come home next weekend, though."

"If you don't I'll be going to St. Paul to see you." He laughed and she laughed with him. "I'll try and come home."

"Okay. Saturday night it is."

"I'll look forward to it."

He walked her to the door and stepping in with her he announced to Herb and Amanda that he'd brought their daughter safely home.

"I'll see you at church tomorrow, Tamar," he said, and left.

Chapter Twenty-one

Sunday morning came too quickly for Tamar. Her heart filled with the events of Saturday night, she was unable to relax immediately after she got in bed, and was still wide awake when the clock chimed the hour of 2:00. What was she going to do with these two men? She already knew that Daniel was out of the picture. She liked him as a friend but her instincts told her that his feelings went deeper than that. Timothy was fun to be with, and yet, she didn't recognize the feelings that she had for him as being love. She wasn't sure. Then there was Paul. What were her feelings for him? Her sensitive side reminded her that someone would most likely get hurt by her actions and that upset her tremendously. She prayed. For twenty minutes she was on her knees. *I'll leave it in God's hands,* she finally rationalized.

In church that morning, Tamar listened carefully to Paul. Timothy usually sat in one of the back pews. She could feel his presence and his eyes probing her back. She could see Maxine seated with her parents a few rows ahead. The ugly scene the day before with Maxine, triggered her mind. Deciding to treat her like nothing had happened, she directed her mind to Paul's sermon.

The phone was ringing in Paul's office. Martin, who was one of the ushers for this Sunday, went to answer it. The voice on the phone divulged that there had been an accident and Timothy was needed at the hospital. Tamar, engrossed in Paul's sermon, was unaware of the happenings behind her. Maxine, hearing a bit of commotion, turned her head and noticed Timothy leaving.

Timothy, on the other hand, was disappointed that he wouldn't be able to see Tamar after the service. He had hopes of chatting with her at length, letting people know that he was interested in Tamar. *Oh well, aiding the sick comes first. It will always have to be this way,* were his thoughts.

After the service ended, Tamar blended into the background. Going to the front, she waited while Tootie was finishing up her music. She had looked for Timothy and found the church void of his presence. *That phone call must have been for him,* she thought.

Herb and Amanda, greeting Reverend Riech at the door, invited him for dinner.

"I gratefully accept your invitation. I'll bring Tamar with me."

They acquiesced and then left.

Paul, performing his last hand shake, went to converse with Tamar. She had walked towards the back of the church after Tootie finished her rendition.

"Hello Tamar. I'm very pleased to see you."

"I'm very thankful to be here."

"I'll get my coat and we can be on our way."

As an after thought he voiced, "Wait a minute, why don't we sing a few songs while we are here and see how we blend?"

"I'd like that," she enthusiastically said.

Paul found a couple of old choir books on the music shelf in back of the church.

Thumbing through the pages he came up with a great number. They again sang to their hearts content.

Dinner over with and Paul and Tamar on their way to St. Paul, they sang more songs. Tamar's heart felt a great tug towards Paul. Yet, she wasn't sure of his feelings. Timothy had already, more or less, announced his.

Paul, meanwhile, was enjoying his time with Tamar immensely. His heart was filled with joy and expectancy of what could be. With sudden realization, the ingredient that captivated his heart with Vivian was her smile and gentleness. These were all great virtues. Enwrapped in a constant partnership with someone, another substance was essential. At

that moment, assessing that knowledgeable thought, Paul realized that love had been the missing integral part with Vivian. What he had felt for her was just a tenderness towards her mental awareness. His senses wide open now, he perceived that he'd found all that was needed in a wife. His heart agreed.

Arriving at her place of residence, he said, "This has been a very satisfying day. I really enjoy being with you."

"I've enjoyed it too."

"Will you be coming home next weekend?"

"I'll try to."

"Could I see you again next Sunday? I'll take you out for dinner. Maybe we can do something Saturday?"

"I can't on Saturday. But dinner on Sunday sounds exciting."

"Okay. Sunday it is. Take good care of yourself," he said as he took hold of her hand and squeezed it. He saw her to the door.

As Paul was driving home, he found it curious that Tamar couldn't see him on Saturday. She hadn't been able to this weekend either. *Well, maybe she goes out to help her Aunt Dorthea,* he thought. Most of his thoughts, as he was driving home, were on Tamar. Paul's thoughts were also passionately charged with his life in Anderville. How fortunate he was to have been granted the duties at St. Peter's.

Sunday afternoon the Niedlich's phone rang.

"Hello, Mrs. Niedlich. Is Tamar still in Anderville?"

"I'm sorry, Dr. Keller, she has already left for St. Paul."

"I was afraid that I had missed her. There was an accident that kept me from seeing her after church."

They talked about that incident for a few minutes and then Timothy asked for Tamar's phone number in St. Paul. Amanda gave it to him and said that she probably wouldn't arrive at her rooming house until about six. Hanging up the phone, Amanda thought, *What in the world is that girl getting herself into. Two men on the string! She needs to make up her mind. This could ruin her reputation!*

Timothy had called Tamar on Sunday evening and they spent time

chatting over the phone.

"I'm sorry that I missed you at church," Timothy verbalized. He went on with, "There was an accident and I had to leave church before the sermon ended."

"I'm sorry to hear that. Was it serious?"

"A farmer was gored by a bull. He was lucky—got himself away from the animal before it really tore into him."

"Well, that's something to be thankful for."

They went on chatting and Timothy again voiced how much he cared about her.

Tamar realized that she had to make up her mind about these two men. She didn't really have the feelings that she should have for Timothy, so she thought. He was fun to be with, he was a perfect gentleman, he was a Christian, but beyond that she couldn't evoke the feelings that should be there for a lifelong commitment. Maybe the feelings would still surface, was her thought on the matter. Paul had not yet asked her for any commitment, she had no idea what was in his mind. She knew that he cared for her, but then, other people cared for her, too. There was another element that had to surface, and that was the element of love. Did he, or was he falling in love with her?

Monday morning Dorthea found that she needed help again. Calling Amanda, she asked for her assistance.

"I'll have my wash finished by noon, Dorthea. I'll come and help you this afternoon." So it was.

Dorthea was doing well with her pregnancy and had recently been in to see Dr. Keller. "He's a fine doctor," she voiced to Amanda.

"Yes, he seems to be. I wish that daughter of ours would make up her mind who she's going to date."

"What's going on?"

Amanda told her about Tamar and her two men. "I don't think that it's a known fact around Anderville yet, so keep it under your hat."

They discussed that for awhile. Dorthea offered, "Well, with Dr. Keller, she'd always have someone near if she got deathly sick."

"Well, that's a way of looking at it, but then, when she really needed

him he'd probably be out on a call for someone else. Having the doctor of her soul close at hand could save her from eternal suffocation."

"How about that, one would be a doctor for her physical well being and the other a doctor for her soul." They were both amused at Tamar and her serious involvements.

Amanda finishing her day at the farm, Dorthea suppling her with some fresh eggs and milk.

Daniel, spied Tamar in the cafeteria on Monday. He sat down beside her.

"I sure missed my walking partner on Sunday," he said.

"I'm sorry for that Daniel, but I will always be going home on weekends from now on—unless we have a snow storm, that is."

"I'm sorry to hear that. You know I care deeply for you, Tamar."

"I know, and I must tell you that as a friend I really appreciate your company."

Letting that thought coagulate for a moment, he then asked, "You don't think that we could arrive at a relationship beyond that?"

"Daniel, I apologize. You need to know that I just don't have the feelings I should have for a lifelong relationship. Believe me, I have earnestly prayed about this."

"I'm sorry too. Well, can we at least eat together?"

"That's okay by me if it doesn't upset you. I just don't want to see you hurt."

So it went. Daniel was very disappointed and Tamar, to some degree, was too.

Tamar, getting her studies in line with the other students once again, was eager to go home on Friday after school. Herb and Amanda, on their way to pick up Tamar, were discussing her situation.

"I just wish Tamar would settle down with one suitor. The way she is carrying on doesn't look respectful," Amanda voiced to Herb.

"Amanda, I wouldn't say that she is carrying on. She has to get a feeling as to which one she can spend a lifetime with. She's doing it the only way that it can be done."

Ending their worrisome topic, they went on to other discussions.

After arriving in Anderville, Tamar, needing some things from the drug store, asked her father to drop her off there, telling him that she would walk home. Herb obliged.

Going into the drug store she noticed Maxine at the counter drinking a soda. Her legs felt a mite weak, but she proposed not to let Maxine disturb her.

"Well, Tamar," Maxine challenged, "What do you have to say for yourself?"

"Hi Maxine. I don't have much to say. Why?"

"You should know that both Dr. Keller and Reverend Riech are just using you."

"What are you talking about? Nobody is using me, Maxine."

As this conversation was going on, Rose was at the counter taking in the entire scene. There was nothing that she could do to avoid it.

"Well, Dr. Keller skated with me at the skating rink before you ever laid eyes on him. And for your information Reverend Riech is dating Mrs. Lute, the librarian.

"Maxine, who I date is actually none of your concern. I don't have to explain away my actions to you," she gently declared to her. "I'm not running after either man, they seek my company. We wholesomely enjoy each other's company."

"Well, neither one of them will ever marry you."

That stung Tamar's heart, but she opted to let it pass. Instead she sat on the other end of the counter and Rose went to wait on her.

"Don't let her upset you, Tamar, but tell me what's going on?"

"In low tones they discussed her involvement with both of the gentlemen.

"You know, Tamar, I told Joe that I wondered why you and Reverend Riech didn't get involved romantically. I think that you two would make a great couple. Joe thought that maybe Reverend Riech felt that he was too busy to start a relationship."

"Well, I really like Reverend Riech but he hasn't declared any of his feelings to me, except that he cared about me. Well that has several implications. My parents, too, care for me, as do my brothers and sisters.

But I must get this sorted out this weekend. I don't want to hurt either one of them."

"I'll say a prayer for you, Tamar."

"Thanks, Rose."

With that said, she picked up the things she needed and left for home. She was deeply hurt however, and didn't want it to show. Walking home she thought, *Reverend Riech and Vivian Lute?* She was stunned. Getting herself home, the coast was clear. She ran to her bedroom and let the tears fall. Now she knew for certain that she was really in love and she knew with whom. *But why is he dating me and Vivian too? That doesn't sound like Paul.* She was sorely wounded.

Maxine on the other hand, couldn't let it rest. It was like a burr that she was sitting on. Picking up the things her mother wanted, she then drove straight to the church. Paul was nowhere around. She left him a message, which she didn't sign, on his office door.

Paul had been at the hospital making his visitations. He stopped to see the man who had been gored by a bull. They had a nice long conversation. Mrs. Oberling was in the hospital, also. He spent time with her, discussing the blood clot in her leg and other things, as well.

Driving homeward he went to the church office first to drop off some mail. Noticing the note on his office door, he picked it up and read, *I wouldn't play the fool if I were you. Everybody knows that Tamar is seeing Dr. Keller.* The words stung his heart. He had an idea that Maxine was the culprit who had so uncouthly drawn his attention to this fact. He sat down at his desk and prayed for a long time about the situation. Then remaining quiet before his God, he felt that God was telling him to excuse the note, continue on with his earthly mission and at long last, present Tamar with his devotion and feelings for her.

He picked up the phone, took the receiver off of its hook, and rang for the operator. He waited for the message, *Number please.* Getting through to the Niedlich home, Amanda answered the phone.

"Hello, Mrs. Neidlich. Pardon me for this intrusion. I'm wondering if Tamar is coming home today?"

"Yes, she is here now. I'll get her for you."

Calling Tamar to the phone, Tamar quickly wiped her tears, patted

some powder over her eyes and hastened to the phone.

On the other end of the line Paul asked, "Could I see you this evening? It's of utmost importance."

"I am anxious to talk with you too, Reverend Riech."

"Okay. We're set then. I'll pick you up at 7:00. Put on your warmest clothes We'll most likely walk for awhile."

As she was getting ready for the outing, Tamar wondered what was going on. *Paul sounded urgent, almost distressed,* she thought. Her heart pained for his discomfort. She, too, cared what happened to him.

Soon Paul picked her up and they were on their way. Not saying a lot to her as they drove, he parked the car by the skating rink. No one was around.

"Do you feel like walking?"

"I'm definitely dressed for it and I do like to walk."

"I remembered that."

He got out of the vehicle and helped Tamar out. Grabbing her mittened hand he directed their path along the side of the skating rink.

This is different, Tamar thought, *he's holding my hand.*

Paul was unusually quiet, a mannerism that did not go unnoticed by Tamar. She kept silent, also.

Finally, coming to a bench, Paul said, "Let's sit for awhile."

They were both seated. She could smell the lingering affects of Old Spice aftershave on him. She herself had splashed on some Coty cologne. The street light was shining above them, stars were in the sky and the moon obliged them with its light, as well. Tamar was almost in anguish over him. It appeared that something was bothering him. Her heart felt heavy. *Is this what it feels like to be in love,* she thought. *I could do without this aspect of love, it hurts too much.*

Paul, with his thoughts finally collected, said, "Tamar, I have great feelings for you. If you could find yourself in a position of the same nature, maybe as time goes by I pray that you can, I would be extremely happy. You don't have to answer me now." He put his arm around her shoulder and went on with, "I know that we are eight years apart in age. You might feel that the span is too great. I'll understand if that is the case."

Tamar listened, a lump growing in her throat. She sat quietly for a moment and then said, "Before I can answer that question, I must tell you that today I heard that you are seeing Vivian Lute. I don't want to get in-between the two of you."

Paul stiffened. He was disturbed. There was no query in his mind. Without a doubt Maxine was at the end of this.

"Tamar, there's nothing to get in-between. I am not dating Vivian. We won't mention any names but it's not hard for me to conjecture who put that thought in your mind. I'm sorry if I've grieved you, Tamar. I know that I am definitely in love with you, although it has taken me awhile to bring that fact to your knowledge. Furthermore, if you would be getting between anyone, it would be between my God and I. You surely realize that God comes first in my life. It will always be that way and it should be that way with you, too. But I promise you, you will always come second. Now it's turn around time. I, too, learned today that you were seeing Dr. Keller."

Putting her thoughts together, she then said, "Yes, I was with him last Saturday night and he has asked me for a date tomorrow night. I know that what I feel for him is only friendship. My heart felt heavy when I learned about you and Vivian and I knew at that moment that what I feel for you is love. As for the age difference, my grandparents had a great life together and they are ten years apart. The age difference won't affect me any. I love you too, Reverend Riech." She laid her head on his chest, listening to the rumbles of his heart.

Enfolding her in both of his arms, he said, "Let God be my witness, I declare to you this day, Tamar, that I love you and will always adore you, comfort you, cherish you and aid you in whatever you need or desire, as God gives me the ability to do so."

He took a deep breath and silently whispered his thanks to God, then taking hold of her chin, lifting it so that he could look into her eyes, he placed a sound, sincere kiss upon her lips. Pulling apart, he hugged her strongly, both arms around her. She wilted in his embrace.

"You have made me very happy," Paul exclaimed, kissing her again. Then he continued with, "And about this reverend business, my name is Paul."

"Okay, Paul. You have won a place in my heart and I will try with God's help, to make you a very good wife."

"There's no doubt in my mind about that. Have you considered what it will be like being a minister's wife? Maybe you spoke too hastily."

"Paul, I haven't even had time to think about it. All of this has come up so fast! No I haven't spoken too hastily. I'll be what God want's me to be, that is your wife. If it's a minister's wife, so be it." Then remembering the biblical story of Ruth and Naomi, she continued with, "I'll go where you go, lodge where you will lodge, your people shall be my people and I will love you wherever we are, and will perform my ascribed duties as your wife. I'll also pray diligently for you and the ministry and for myself, too."

Paul was so moved that he hugged her and kissed her one more time. Then he said,"Well, we'll need to talk about this 'minister's wife' business again sometime. But for now I just want to linger in your presence and soak up all of this love."

"I am so fortunate. God is so good!" Tamar exclaimed.

"We know that He is."

They sat quietly, Paul's arms around her, they were bathed in devotion, love and thankfulness.

Chapter Twenty-two

Paul and Tamar had a lot of things to discuss. Leaving the bench and coldness behind, they opted for warmer surroundings. Paul, against his better judgment, decided that the parsonage would be a quiet place to talk and plan. At his home no one would overhear their future plans. Tamar was eager to see the house, and they reckoned that should anyone discover that they had been alone in Paul's home, they didn't have to explain their actions to anyone but God. He was their Master, it was to God alone that they needed to bring an account of their actions. This house soon would become her home and she was very eager to see it.

Putting on the coffee pot, Paul asked Tamar to make herself comfortable. "May I see the upstairs?" Tamar just realized that after all of these years of living in Anderville, and being a member of St. Peter's, she had never been through the entire house. Paul took her on a tour of the whole house. Her mind was whirling.

"How will I ever be able to keep up all of this space?" she questioned of Paul.

"I have faith in you, Tamar, and besides that, have you forgotten that I am a good house cleaner, too."

Standing at one of the bedroom doors, on their tour of the upstairs, Tamar stated, "This would be a lovely room for girls."

"Perhaps one of ours," Paul replied as he put his arm around her.

She blushed and said, "Maybe."

The tour behind them, drinking their coffee, they discussed details about their upcoming wedding. Paul, looking at Tamar, could see her enthusiasm. He, too, was thrilled but tried to contain his sense of balance.

"I know that all of this is going to interfere with your schooling. Do you think that we can be married as soon as this school year has ended?"

She took hold of his hand and answered, "Yes, it certainly will interfere." She chuckled. "And yes, we can be married in June. How about the third Sunday of June?"

"Good! I'll have vacation coming about then and we can plan a short honeymoon."

Enthusiasm reigned high as their planning went on. Finishing their coffee at the kitchen table, Paul escorted her to the living room and they were seated on the sofa. Together they talked of their lives as one, going over wedding plans as well. Paul held her hand occasionally, stealing a kiss now and then. He revered his Heavenly Father also, by silently giving Him thanks for this wonderful gift. When he noticed the waning moon in the far distant sky, their night abruptly ended. Realizing that he had kept Tamar out at an unthinkable hour, he hurried her home.

Yawning and stretching as he got up the next morning, Paul was filled with elation. He sent a prayer of thanksgiving to his Master, and hurried his breakfast on. This was going to be a fulfilling day and a busy one. Above all else, he wanted to go to Hutchinson first to pick out a ring for Tamar. After all, he wanted everyone to know that Tamar had been spoken for, that he had won her heart. He spent time in his devotions with his Heavenly King for he had much to be thankful for. The other pressing thing that he had to do this day was to talk with Timothy. Tamar would not be seeing Timothy this evening.

The two had talked about her date with Timothy and both had decided that Paul should talk to him instead of Tamar. Paul, very humble and very happy, hastened on with his duties.

Tamar slept in that morning. It was 2:30 when she claimed her bed that night—actually that morning. Giving her praises to God as she awakened, she was still walking in a cloud, yet ever so thankful and very humble.

Ultimately, going downstairs to help her mother and Tootie with the household chores, she spoke to her mother, "Mom, I have finally solved

the problem with these two men."

"Thank heavens! What happened?"

Tamar went on to tell her mother how Maxine actually brought the situation to a head. She spared no details. Tootie and Amanda were both engrossed in her every word.

Amanda realizing that Paul needed a wife, asked, "Don't tell me that we're going to have a hurried wedding here?"

"You'll have some time. The wedding is for June 16th."

Remembering that her mother was a great seamstress she asked if she could make her wedding dress.

"Well, if both of you girls help around the house I should be able to finish it in time. We better get to Hutchinson soon to pick out the material." They decided to do that the next weekend.

Paul, having finished his mission in Hutchinson, hurried back to Anderville to look up Timothy. He tried his office. He wasn't there. Going to the hospital, he inquired at the front desk if Timothy might be there. He wasn't there either. Taking out time in his busy day, he stopped to see Mrs. Oberling. He was pleased to hear that she was mending well. Then, driving to Timothy's home he noticed that his car was parked in front, which gave an indication that he was at home.

Timothy, surprised to see Paul at the door, welcomed him in.

"What brings you about this morning?" he asked.

Paul spared no punches, coming forth with, "Well, I'm not sure how you are going to take this Timothy, but my intentions are good."

"Well, save me the agony. What's going on?"

"Tamar and I are engaged to be married. I wanted to be the first to tell you."

Timothy was stunned. Paul went on with, "I know that you two had a date for tonight. Of course you realize that under the present circumstances that cannot happen."

Gaining his composure, he said, "Well, well, so the best man won."

"I'm not saying that I'm the best man, I only pray that I will be a good husband for her."

"I'm sure that you will be, Paul."

"Thank you, Timothy." Taking a deep breath, he continued with, "Would you do me the honors of being my groomsman?"

Timothy hadn't expected all of this to take place on this day. He thought for only a moment and happily said, "It will be my privilege."

Paul returned to his home, fixed a late lunch for himself and spent some time in prayer. Realizing that he had work on his desk at the church office to do, he went to finish up with those details and then gave thought to his sermon for the next day.

His sermon was based on Matthew 25, starting with verse 31. He concentrated on verse 40: And the King will answer them, "*Truly, I say to you, as you did it to one of the least of these my brethren, you did it to me." He pondered that significant implication. So if I do something good for my fellowman*, he thought, *than it's like I am doing it for Jesus. If I choose to do some evil deed to someone that has to mean it's like slapping Jesus in the face or worse.*

Although he had studied this scripture before, the connotation came through more clearly this time. He was both awed and alarmed at those words that Jesus spoke. He went on with his reviewing.

The Niedlich women finished up their Saturday baking and cleaning, and Tamar felt that they should invite Paul for supper. Amanda was in agreement. Tamar was able to reach Paul at the church and he readily accepted.

"After supper I'd like to take you out for awhile. We'll make this a short night, seeing how we were up so late last night. I need to be refreshed for Sunday morning, too. See, you are getting a taste of being a minister's wife already. Your life will never be the same. Are you sure that you wouldn't like to change your mind?"

"I think that I can adjust, Paul. And no, I do not wish to change my mind. I'll reluctantly release you early tonight. I do realize that it's for the most important performances of all; that of being about our Father's business."

Paul, arriving at the Niedlich home, had his speech prepared for Herb. Amanda warmly welcomed him in with a big smile, saying, "I hear that your intentions are to become part of this family."

"Mrs. Niedlich, I'd be very pleased if you would accept me as your son-in-law."

"You are welcomed to the family and I can't think of anyone that I would rather have as a husband for my daughter."

Paul thought, *that was easy, now for my audience with Herb.*

Amanda said, "Herb's in the living room, just make yourself at home."

Herb rose and shock hands with Paul. "What's this I hear?" he questioned.

"Herb, with your permission I'd like to make Tamar my wife. I promise to always love and cherish her and treat her with greatest respect, which is her God given right."

"You certainly have my permission. A father can't ask for more than that. God bless your union." Herb again shook his hand and patted him on the back.

They went on discussing the ins and outs of Paul and Tamar's life together, going on with the weather and gardening soon to be.

"Yes, we'll most likely be putting in a garden. I'll have to ask my wife-to-be about that though," Paul chuckled as he voiced that.

Herb laughed too and was keen on Paul's answer. *At least he's going to involve Tamar in his decisions. That should avoid a few squabbles.*

After supper Paul and Tamar drove to the skating rink to watch the skaters for awhile. They sat upon the same bench where they, the night before, had spoken their love for each other.

Maxine was in full swing. She avoided Paul and Tamar. Timothy was her target for the night. He skated one number with her and then went to talk with Paul and Tamar, congratulating Tamar. "I know that he'll make a good husband for you," he opined. Their chatter was filled with laughter and banter of one thing or another, mostly about the lives of Paul and Tamar together.

As he knuckled Paul in the arm, laughing, Timothy asked, "Are you going to let Tamar write your sermons, Paul?"

"Paul chuckled and said, as he hugged her, "Well, she probably could."

"I'll leave that work to Paul. That's his calling. I'll have my hands busy keeping up the house," Tamar inserted.

Paul soon reasoned that they should leave for warmer corners. This was to be the last skating party of the winter. Tamar felt a pang of nostalgia, hating to see the end of the skating season, although she was eager for the spring flowers to appear.

Maxine set her cap for Timothy again and he became offended that he couldn't just skate and enjoy himself. He removed his skates and went home.

Paul and Tamar on their way to Spruce Island, chatted away about Tamar's life as the wife of a minister.

"You'll probably have to learn how to quilt, Tamar."

"I'd rather leave that for my mother, but I guess I can learn. If it doesn't get more complicated than that, I'll survive."

"There is another element that could cause conflict. My duties also include counseling members. This could be a problem, especially if I'm called to counsel women. You'll have to put a lot of trust in me."

"I will always trust you, Paul."

"Like a doctor, things said to me must be confidential. I won't always be able to discuss issues with you."

"I understand."

Once in Spruce Island, Paul parked the car and turned off the lights. Taking the ring from his pocket, he held it before Tamar and said, "This is a token of my affection for you, Tamar. Thank you for accepting my heart and my life."

He placed the ring on her finger, lifted her face to his and placed a kiss upon her lips. She was so startled and surprised by all of this, unspoken words got tangled and caught in her throat. Mumbling incoherently, eventually getting her bearings together, she said, "Thank you, Paul. I'll cherish your gift and your words always." She dared a kiss.

It was rather dark and she couldn't see the ring too well. Inside the café they found a quiet booth. Tamar was eager to inspect her ring but waited until they had ordered their hot cocoa.

"It is beautiful, Paul! Did you pick this out by yourself?"

"I did indeed."

"You did a fabulous job!" As an after thought she smiled at him and

added, "You'll make someone a good husband someday."

"I plan on doing that," he said as he laughed and hugged her.

The next morning Paul directed his sermon to no one in particular, although he felt that there was a need for it.

He noticed Maxine squirming in her seat. *Well, maybe it hit home,* he thought. Not that he particularly aimed it at her. Not to pass judgment, Paul was aware that the scripture was written for him as well.

The Becks and Carl and Sophia, sat beside the Niedlichs, all eager to see Tamar's ring. Amanda had phoned Dorthea on Saturday and had given her the news. So by the end of the service most people knew that Paul and Tamar were engaged. Some of the members had already seen her ring before church started and a good many of them were happily surprised. They had no idea that their minister had been courting.

Maxine, receiving that bit of news, was beside herself. She left the church and sat in the family car, waiting for the rest of the family. The service over with and the Schmit family on their way home, Maxine said, "I'm not going to that church anymore. I'll join the church in Spruce Island. I'll soon be making my home there anyway."

Gloria had an idea why Maxine seemed to be upset and she let it pass, agreeing with her, if that was her desire.

Paul and Tamar were congratulated by everyone, everyone but Maxine, that is. Many questions were asked of them, like, "Would Tamar quit school?"

Their answer to that was, "We haven't even discussed that issue yet."

Finally the church emptied and Tamar waited for Paul to remove his robe and put his overcoat on. He never wore a hat. The only time that his head was covered was during extremely cold weather and when he went skating, of course.

Although Herb and Amanda had invited Paul and Tamar for dinner, they wanted to spend the afternoon by themselves. Paul had advised Herb that from now on he would be glad to take Tamar back to school and would pick her up on Friday afternoons unless some unforeseen calamity befell him or one of his flock. Herb was very willing.

Paul, getting Tamar to agree, took her to dinner in St. Paul at the café

where he had taken her before. They talked endlessly on their way over and sang some songs too.

Paul asked, "How important is school to you?"

"I really had my heart set on it."

"How about being my wife first and later on you can finish?"

"Well, maybe I could go back this fall and get at least one more year behind me."

"We'll see how that works out. You might become a mother and that would invade a good deal of your time."

"I wouldn't call it an invasion. I would love being a mother!"

So it was decided. They would take this small problem to their Heavenly Father and let him take care of this matter.

Paul also had a future vision. He felt that it would be better if they sought another congregation after a few more years in Anderville. Especially since he had married into the congregation. Tamar agreed. No one would be able to accuse them of showing partiality to the relatives if they were not part of St. Peter's. This was a good idea.

They talked about going to Milwaukee to spend their honeymoon. Tamar was eager to meet his relatives.

After dinner Paul drove to a park that he was familiar with. Snow still blanketing the earth, didn't deter them one bit. Walking around the park, Tamar's hand in Paul's, they were both deliriously in love. Finding a bench, they sat for a short while. Paul ever cognizant of Tamar's health, put his arm around her, holding her close to keep her warm.

They moved on. Going to a café they ordered a sandwich, pie and coffee.

The afternoon, being swallowed by the sun's disappearance, made the couple aware that it was time to take Tamar to her rooming house. Paul didn't want to leave her and Tamar was reluctant to say goodbye. He held her close, getting a supply of kisses to last the rest of the week.

"I'll call you during the week," he said.

"I'll be waiting," she answered.

Chapter Twenty-three

Several weeks went by. Winter was transporting itself to another range. Fields of melting snow were becoming a big nuisance, a quagmire of a headache. Mud clung to overshoes and wheels. But through it all, women were eager to get out in their gardens. Good Friday was just two weeks away. Potato planting time was upon them. Hopefully, the sun would do its work and dry out the fields before then.

Paul, true to his word, was very eager to pick up Tamar from school, taking her back on Sunday afternoons. Paul's jubilation was obvious by the wide grin on his face as he watched Tamar's prudent departure out of the college door. Enthusiastically walking towards her, wrapping her in his arms, he hugged her proudly. His lips meeting her lips, their kiss was tender, kisses that had been nonexistent for most of the week. Taking her suitcase from her, they walked to the car. She was as eager and happy to see him as he was to see her. These trips back and forth to St. Paul each weekend brought the two in closer unity, and provided the idyllic time to discuss their future oneness.

Paul dropped her off at the drug store on this Friday, as she had requested. He himself knowing that he still had visitations to make at the hospital. In parting he said, "Your mom invited me for supper so I'll see you later." She thanked him for dropping her off and waved to him as he drove away.

Walking into the drug store, she sat down at the counter and waited for Rose to wait on her. Seeing Tamar, Rose became very eager to talk to her. Finishing with a customer and not another customer in sight, she hurried to Tamar.

"You'll never guess who is going to beat you to the altar."

"Who? Dr. Keller and Maxine?"

"Well, you've got it half way right. Maxine is getting married. She's going to marry this bus driver on Easter Sunday."

Tamar was stunned. "Paul doesn't know about that. At least he hasn't said anything to me."

"They aren't getting married here. They are getting married in Mankato."

"What'a you know? In Mankato?"

"He's from Mankato."

"Well she's been going to church in Spruce Island."

"I heard that. Guess she didn't like the idea of Reverend Riech marrying you."

Tamar's thought was on how sorry she felt for Maxine. She then said, "Humm," going on with, "Rose, the reason I stopped by is to ask if you would be my bridesmaid. Tootie is going to be my maid-of-honor."

With great enthusiasm she answered, "Tamar, I would love to!"

Just then another customer came in and the conversation ended.

"See you later," Tamar voiced as she left.

Supper at the Niedlich's home was joyous. Everyone was excited about the up-coming wedding. Conversation wound around Tamar's new home also. New curtains were on her mind, and she voiced that. Paul understood that women had their quirks of this nature, even his mother. Amanda suggested that they make them. On went their ideas and suggestions.

Supper dishes cleaned and put away, Tamar and Paul were off to doing their own entertaining.

As they left Amanda said, "Paul you're invited for supper tomorrow also. We'd love to have you for the evening, too. Bill and Dorthea and my folks will be here again."

Paul looked at Tamar and putting his arm around her, said, "Once we get set up for housekeeping, we'll return the favors. Thanks for the invitation."

The couple on their way out of the Niedlich establishment, thought to

go to the bowling alley to watch the bowlers for awhile. On the way, Tamar, her mind on what Rose had relayed to her, said, "Maxine is getting married on Easter Sunday."

"Really! to whom?"

"This bus driver that she's been seeing."

Thinking for a moment, he then said, "I feel badly about this. I pray that she knows what she is doing."

"We all need to pray for her. I heard that she was upset when she found out that we were getting married."

"It's too bad. She could be a very nice person if she would only let God do her directing. I feel badly, too, since I really enjoy her brother, Philip, in my confirmation class."

Feeling sorry for Paul, she said, "Better days lie ahead Paul. We'll pray about this issue."

With that said the discussion was dropped. Gossiping was not a natural thing for him to engage in.

Once at the bowling alley, Paul found a table for them and they both ordered a hot cocoa.

Rose and Joe were bowling along with her folks, Laura and Martin. Martin spotted them, waved and invited them over. They finished their hot cocoa and then joined them. There was much for them to discuss and Paul needed to speak with his friend, Martin, anyway.

Shaking hands with Laura, Rose and Joe, he then said, "Martin, you're just the person that I want to talk to."

"Well, here I am," Martin responded.

"I would be honored if you would be my best man."

Just then it was Martin's turn to bowl. He took his position and hit a strike. Everyone cheered and Martin returned to Paul to answer his inquiry.

"I'd be honored to be your best man, Paul." They shook hands, Martin clapping him on the back. Talking on about Paul's ministerial duties, the two were keeping the conversation flowing.

When Rose was not tied up with her bowling ball, she and Tamar talked about the upcoming wedding.

"What are your colors going to be, Tamar?" Rose asked.

"I'm going for blue and yellow. Tootie want's to wear the yellow. Is blue okay for you?"

"I love blue!"

The two young ladies were all excited and occasionally Laura was able to get in a few words.

"Tell your mother that I'd be glad to help if she is in need," Laura said to Tamar.

"She probably will be. I'll tell her that you offered to help."

After bowling the six people went to the café for refreshments. Great conversation easily rolled from their lips. Martin was telling tales of his childhood, his audience laughing gleefully. Paul added to it with some of his adolescent capers.

Soon it was time to end the evening and Paul drove his betrothed home. It had been a fun evening. They cuddled for a minute or two and then Paul said, "I'll see you tomorrow. I love you."

"I'm deeply in love with you."

He tweaked her nose, kissed her and walked her to the door.

Tamar, still on cloud nine, waltzed through her chores the next day. She had it in her mind that a way to a man's heart is through his stomach; she wanted to make a special treat for the evening.

"Mom, can I make those good "swirley" cookies for tonight? You know, the chocolate and vanilla ones that taste almost like candy.

"It's okay with me. They are time consuming."

"I don't mind. I'll make some oatmeal cookies too."

Amanda gave her the reigns and Tootie and Amanda did the house cleaning. Eugene was in the house looking at comic books and Amanda thought she had a good job for him.

"Eugene, come, you can help us get ready for our company. You can dust the dining room furniture."

"Ah, that's girls stuff."

"It never hurts a man to get his hands into dusting."

She showed him the ropes and he reluctantly took the dust cloth.

"I can't wait until Ruth is big enough to do this."

Amanda, as she was dusting the living room, watched him.

"Ah, ah. Do it good, Eugene. Any job worth doing is worth doing well."

Like a turtle, he eased his neck into his chest and started over.

The work and cookie baking went on.

That evening, with an arm full of hymnals, Paul arrived for supper. Tamar met him at the door. Taking the hymnals from him she put them on the organ stool, and then took his coat. With a warm hug and a kiss upon her lips, he then greeted the rest of the family. Bill and Dorthea and the grandparents came shortly after supper, Dorthea bringing some milk and eggs for Amanda. Dorthea's short stature accentuated the largeness of her pregnancy. She still had a few months to go.

First of all, the ladies were eager to see how Amanda was doing on the making of Tamar's wedding dress. It was made of white rayon with an overlay of lace to the bodice, lace sleeves, fitting tightly at the wrist and coming to a point on her hand, pearl buttons securing the opening. Amanda was almost finished with it. Hand sewing would finish up the project. The women "ooh'd" and "aah'd" over Amanda's intricate work.

Tootie warmed up the organ. Everyone found a place to sit and Tamar made sure that Paul was seated beside her.

"This is wonderful," Dorthea said. "We've missed your presence, Tamar and Paul."

Grandma, answering with her usual German saying, said, "Ach du lieber, *oh you lovely,*" Going on with, " We sure have. Now the flock is complete…for us here in Anderville, anyway."

They sang to their hearts content. Soon Herb got out his violin and with Tootie at the organ, Dorthea and Bill waltzed to, "My Wild Irish Rose."

Paul, not one for dancing, did try a few steps with Tamar. It was frowned upon for the ministers to dance—frowned upon for members also, although some couples did enjoy dancing. It was believed to be one of Satan's tools. In this private setting Paul obliged Tamar with a dance, holding her close to his heart.

Lunch was served and Amanda let it be known that Tamar had baked the cookies.

Paul praised her for her effort, saying, "You'll make someone a good wife some day."

Everyone laughed and Tamar answered him with, "That someone will be you, won't it?" She had a devilish grin on her face. He grabbed her, hugged her and said, "You're not getting away from me."

Chapter Twenty-four

In the midst of Easter Lilies and palm branches, Paul in his pulpit, declared Christ risen from the dead. This was a gift to all, the free gift of a life that is everlasting. Christ himself had purchased that life for everyone by his cruel death and divine resurrection. Paul elaborated on that point. His exuberance caught hold in the hearts of his congeners, happy faces approvingly smiled at him. Paul went on to say that no sin was so great that God would not forgive it. Even the thief on the cross was taken to heaven, he announced. More than likely the man had never been baptized. He had just, at that moment, accepted Jesus and that was the necessary element. One might say that this was his baptism; the great baptism of Jesus' words. Paul put good thoughts into their minds.

The choir blended perfectly on, "Christ The Lord Is Risen Today." Tootie had outdone herself with music for this great occasion, as well. Tamar was much too busy to take time to practice for the church services. She would wait until things settled down a bit.

Paul exuberantly greeted each and every person as they left the church. Timothy eagerly shook his hand thanking him for the wonderful sermon that he had given.

"It is the work of our Savior. He should be the one that we all thank," Paul replied.

"You are right and I will do that. Stop over if you have time this week."

"I'll be sure to do that," Paul answered.

Both Rose and Joe were amongst the congregators. They both wholeheartedly greeted him. Paul pointed out that married life seemed to be agreeing with them.

Joe said, "You'll soon be able to know how great it is! We're both very happy."

"I'm happy for you, and yes, I'll soon be amongst the married population. I'm looking forward to it," Paul answered them. He went on greeting the happy throng.

Tamar went home with her parents to help get the Easter dinner on. The grandparents and Becks would be their guests along with Margie, Rufus and his girlfriend, Arlene, who came for Easter and were staying with Sophia and Carl. So much excitement going on that Tamar had a hard time keeping herself at an even keel.

Guests gathering at the Niedlich's were all eager to greet one another, and to dig into the food placed upon the dining room table. Dorthea and Grandma had brought food to help supplement the meal. There was a big juicy ham, corn pudding, sweet potatoes covered with marshmallows and brown sugar, home canned beans with bacon and onion, mashed potatoes and gravy, Grandma's sweet and dill pickles, homemade rolls, pies of all kinds. Laughter spread over the table. Congratulations circled around Tamar and Paul, and also Rufus and Arlene. Their wedding would be coming up before the end of the year. Rufus had met Arlene through church activities in Fort Wayne.

After dinner clean up, Paul and Tamar bid everyone goodbye and left for St. Paul. Tamar was so overjoyed by the events of the day that she slid over next to Paul, hoping that she wasn't dreaming. It had been a great gathering. They talked about how things would appear next Easter. "Or even this Christmas," Tamar voiced.

"I hadn't even thought that far ahead," Paul answered. "We will be together; that's the most important factor. I love you, Marlee."

He had taken to calling her Marlee, taking the last part of Tamar and adding the "le" from her middle name, Leona. She rather liked the "twist" that he put on her name, mainly because it was a part of him.

"Not as much as I love you!" she answered.

"Now wait a minute. I'm bigger than you are. Because there is more of me than there is of you, I contain more love."

Tamar laughed and said, "Okay. If you want to look at it that way then I'm the lucky one. You love me lots."

"I'll say amen to that." He sent a wink her way.

As they neared St. Paul, Tamar noticed an elderly Negro lady carrying a load of something. She was plodding along, looking very weak and worn. A young boy came to meet her and took some of her load.

"They do have a hard load to carry," Tamar absent mindlessly said.

"And whom are you speaking of?"

"The Negroes."

Paul looked over at the woman and said, "Yes, they do have. It's their faith that sustains them."

"I've read of some of the things that happened to them when they were slaves. Carrying their heavy burdens and sorrows as they did, and they still came out of the ordeal believing in God, and perhaps more fervently. They are remarkable! I think that they will inherit the better part of heaven for all of their heartache."

"The Bible doesn't say that, but the majority of them seem to be strong believers."

They went to the park again and walked. It was a beautiful sunny day. Tamar, her arm linked in Paul's, thought that she was the luckiest person in the world. Paul just simply relished the day, thanking God again for his good fortune.

Around about this time in Mankato, surrounded by Easter lilies, carnations and white gladiolas, Maxine's arm was resting in the crook of her father's arm as he two-stepped her down the white carpeted aisle. The organ was spewing out the wedding march, "A Midsummer Night's Dream," as the flower girl strewed apple petals down the aisle. Maxine was a beauty in her wedding dress of white lace and chiffon, that looked very expensive. Her dark hair was professionally combed, her makeup perfect and her nails had been painted a rose color. The long train trailing behind Maxine, shimmered in its hesitancy to ascend to the altar.

Standing with the Reverend Moss were the groom, Lawrence Johns; the best man, his brother, Orville; the groomsman, Maxine's brother, Phillip, and the ring bearer, Maxine's cousin, Steven Schmidt.

The bridesmaid was a sister to the groom; the maid-of-honor, Maxine's sister, Geraldine. The flower girl was the groom's niece.

The wedding proceeded, all seemed in perfect harmony until Lawrence went to kneel for the blessing and noticed that in his haste to dress for his wedding, he had forgotten to zip up his pants. He pulled over the jacket and for the most part, felt that he had it concealed.

Their vows spoken, the couple smiled broadly and walked to the rear of the church to greet their friends and relatives.

As luck would have it, no one noticed the groom's misfortune. A few of St. Peter's members were in attendance. Paul and the Niedlichs had not been invited.

Now that the days were warmer, Ruth eagerly took to the outdoors. She felt that she had been shut up too long. Out riding her tricycle, she rode up and down the sidewalk. Her instruction was that she was not to cross the street. Seeing Loretta, the lady that the town had labeled a "sinner," raking her yard, Ruth stopped to watch from across the street.

Loretta noticed and said, "Hello, little one. How are you?"

"Hi. . . I'm fine," Ruth said, as the wheels in her mind were turning. She knew that she wasn't to cross the street, but did so anyway. Also remembering what her family had talked about concerning Loretta, she cast heed to the winds and asked, "Why does that man always come to your house?"

Loretta was a bit startled, then realizing how it must look to others, said, "Why, Honey, that's my brother. He has trouble with arthritis and I put warm packs on his back every day so that he can work. That's the only thing that helps him."

"Oh."

"What's your name?"

"My name is Ruth."

They talked on for awhile and then Ruth hurried on home.

Loretta and her husband had recently moved to Anderville and the town's people knew little about them. Loretta's brother visited her every day, coming from a town south of Anderville. He was a night watchman and when his stint ended, he drove to Anderville to have his sister place warm packs on his spine.

That evening at the supper table, Ruth let the cat out of the bag. She liked the nice lady across the street and meaning to defend her, said, "That man has a sore back."

"What man?" Amanda asked.

"That man that goes over to the lady across the street."

"Have you been over there Ruth?"

"I was on my tricycle."

"You were told not to cross the street, Ruth," Herb stated.

"I just wanted to watch her."

"What else did she tell you?" John asked.

The entire story came out and the family sat in a mortified judgment seat that they had allowed to happen.

Finally, Amanda said, "Things are not always as they look. We must be careful what seeds we plant into the minds of others."

The family sheepishly agreed.

Although Herb felt that Ruth should have been punished for her disobedience, the lesson that the family learned compensated for punishment.

Chapter Twenty-five

Vivian felt that she was a very fortunate lady. She had thousands of books at the town library at her disposal. Taking one home on Friday night to read, she became very engrossed in the tale and had a hard time putting it aside. She was upstairs in her bedroom in bed, reading. Realizing that she would never get to the interesting part that evening, she reluctantly put it down. Looking at her bedside clock, it was 12:15. Her lips were parched. A drink of water would soothe her throat.

Donning her robe she was tying it about her on her way down the steps when she missed the third step, catching just the edge of it and went down. Her foot crumpled beneath her. She was in pain. Trying to stand on it caused more pain. Knowing that she had carelessly broken it, and also noting the hour, she didn't want to disturb anyone. She decided to wait it out until morning. Hobbling to the bathroom, Vivian got herself a glass of water and took a pain pill that she had left over from a bad wisdom tooth. Limping back to her bed, she elevated her leg on extra pillows and tried to sleep.

On this same evening Bill Beck had a council meeting at church. Paul, ever the good host, brought the meeting to order by telling some humorous tale to get the men, who were usually tired from a full days work in the fields, at attention. The humorous tale, one about his childhood, brought laughter in abundance. The meeting proceeded.

Bill off to the meeting, left Dorthea home alone with Dorene. Having put Dorene down for the night, Dorthea was reading a magazine. Soon the sandman tapped her on the shoulder, too. Bed was a good place to be.

Anderville being a safe area to live in, the door was never locked. They also had a cattle dog, Bullet. Bullet, being a very friendly dog, wasn't much of a bullet.

Soon Dorthea heard the door open and someone entering the house. Looking at the clock, Dorthea was surprised that Bill was home already, and was even more surprised that she hadn't heard the car, nor did Bullet bark.

"Is that you, Bill?"

No answer. Dorthea in her nightgown, got out of bed and went to the kitchen. She was aghast at the stranger standing in her home. Throwing her hands to her face, she stifled the scream in her throat that lay ready to disgorge. The stranger looked disoriented, his hair disheveled.

"What are you doing here?"

"I want something to eat."

"Where are you from?"

"Out there."

Dorthea could tell that he seemed misplaced and had no sense of where he was or who he was. Pulling herself together, she could see that he didn't seem to be dangerous, but she was cautious.

"I'll get you something to eat and find you a place to stay."

She fixed him a sandwich, gave him a glass of milk and while he was busy eating she phoned Pat Murphy, the town constable, giving him her plight.

"I'll be right there," he volunteered.

Bill came home soon after the constable got there. He was stupefied by all of the action at his house.

Constable Murphy was busy with the offender when Bill walked in. Acknowledging one another with a greeting, Murphy then clued him in on the happenings.

No amount of words could bring the man to tell where he was from. It was a mystery to them. They finally decided that he had walked away from some institution, walking, and had probably hitched hiked, too, and landed in Anderville. The constable said he'd see that he was taken care of.

After Murphy and the intruder left, Dorthea said, "He scared me to

death! I'm lucky I didn't have my baby right then and there!"

"I'm thankful that you are okay," Bill said as he let out a relieved breath.

He folded her in his arms, waiting for her to calm down. They went off to bed, very thankful that things had gone as well as they did.

Early morning Vivian's foot started to throb. Her endurance level was about shattered, but she wanted to try and wait until a decent hour, and went for another pain killer.

Tossing and turning until about 6:00, she couldn't bear the pain anymore. She hobbled to the phone and called her neighbors, Ted and Arlene Boyd. They both came to her aid.

Arlene took hold of the situation and voiced, "You'll need a doctor. We'll take you to the hospital since the doctor's office isn't open yet."

They helped her to their car, got her situated and drove to the Anderville hospital.

The hospital staff, seeing someone in a difficult situation, took a wheelchair out to assist.

The staff made Vivian as comfortable as possible while the head nurse put in a call to Dr. Keller.

They went about their business, getting needed information from Vivian.

Soon the doctor arrived. He spoke kindly to her as she explained to him the situation that she had gotten herself into.

"You need not have waited. I'm on call 24 hours a day. We still have Dr. Myers with us too," Dr. Keller relayed to her.

He put her injured ankle in a cast that went to her knee and advised that she stay off of her feet for the next two days. Crutches became an appendage.

"Come back to see me in five weeks, unless there is a problem, of course."

Vivian thanked him and using the crutches, went on her way.

Tamar was home for the weekend again. Saturday morning, leaving Amanda and Tootie to get things ready for Dorthea's baby shower, she

drove to the parsonage to get her future home ready for her life with Paul.

She spent time cleaning out the kitchen cupboards, putting down new shelf liner. Paul had lived here almost a year and it was ready for a thorough cleaning. After that chore she spring-cleaned the bathroom, putting up the new curtains that Amanda had made.

Paul came home for lunch and hugged Tamar, thanking her for her achievements.

"I like the curtains, Marlee," he offered.

The blue does brighten up the room," she answered.

They had lunch, after which Tamar cleaned up the kitchen, then went home to help with the shower which would be held at the Niedlich home that afternoon.

Friends and relatives gathering for the baby shower, were all eager to visit with one another. Everyone was anxious to know about the uninvited visitor at the Beck farm.

Dorthea told the tale, telling all that the man had walked away from a mental institute. Everyone was a bit skeptical about life in Anderville if such could happen.

Amanda said, "It's just a freak thing and the likes will probably never happen again. He could have gone to any one of the other towns around us. I'll not lose any sleep over it but I will lock my doors." That sounded sensible to all of them.

It had been a great gathering and many nice gifts were given for this lucky baby.

That evening Paul picked up Tamar and they went walking in the park. The skating rink, which actually was a pond, was glimmering and water lilies were floating about as birds rested on their large leaves. It was a beautiful sight.

Paul, walking near water, was reminded of his love for fishing. He said, "I'll have to take you fishing."

"I'm not fond of fishing, but if it means that I will be near you, I'll consent."

He hugged her to him and said, "Thank you. I do love to fish."

"I'll fish with you if you'll shop with me."

"That's a great arrangement!"

And so it would be. They walked on and then went for a treat, after which Paul took her home. They talked for a few minutes more and then Paul reluctantly released her to her own bearings. After all, they would have more togetherness the next day.

Chapter Twenty-six

Weeks went by. The people of Anderville went about their customary occupations and were also busy putting in their gardens. Paul and Tamar had been busy putting in a garden also. Tamar had the parsonage cleaned and ready for her to occupy as soon as the wedding was performed, which was drawing near. Some of her things had already been transported to their new place, like the cedar chest that her parents had given her for graduation and the maple rocking chair that came from the Niedlich grandparents. She was eager to start taking up housekeeping.

Things had been going well with the young couple, and one day Paul busied himself helping Tamar plant radishes and carrots. An end of garden hose lay on the ground near by. As Paul looked at it, he first thought it to be a snake. An idea struck him. Tamar, bent over, was scattering seeds in their rightful rows. Paul picked up the remnant and slyly wiggled it between her feet. Screaming like a stuck hog, she threw up her hands, and seeds scattered every which way in the garden.

Paul instantly went to her and hugged her. "I didn't mean to frighten you that badly. I'm sorry, Tamar."

"Paul, you're usually more serious than this. What ever enticed you to play a trick on me?"

Still holding her he said, "You are the one that makes me clown around. I'm truly sorry. I just love you so much."

"You needn't be sorry," she said, as she looked into his eyes. "You do need to be a little jesting at times, too. I'll survive."

He hugged her and then made an attempt to help pick up the seeds, with some sod mixed in, of course, and plant them where they were meant to be.

Paul enjoyed having Tamar around and gardening was a challenge for both of them.

Vivian was having a difficult time with her cast before the five weeks were up and resolved to go see Dr. Keller. Dressed in appropriate attire, she looked sensational in her aqua two pieced dress. Her hair was neatly styled.

"Good morning," Timothy said as he entered the small room. My, you look much better than the last time that I saw you. What seems to be the problem?"

"I hate to be a complainer, but the cast is hurting my ankle."

"Well, let's see what we can do about that."

Observing the problem, the cast was probably putting pressure on an area of her ankle. Cupping his chin with his right hand, he thought for a moment. The cast needed to be removed, was his analysis. Getting busy with that, he noted the area in question. The cast indeed, was causing pressure. A new one was necessary. As he applied it, this gave them a chance to visit a bit.

"I hear that you are the librarian," Timothy said.

"Yes, I am. I'm anxious to get back to my job." "I can understand that."

They went on talking and Timothy was seized by her smile. He thought, *some lucky man will be the recipient of that smile quite soon, I'm sure. And on top of all of that, she's very intelligent.*

"I'll see you again in two and a half weeks," he ordered.

She smiled beautifully and said, "I'll be here. I'm anxious to get back to work." He bid her a good day and she left.

On Monday, May 20th, Dorthea realized that this was going to be an important day. Mother nature had been indicating the last couple of hours that she was soon to become a mother again. She readied herself.

After dropping Dorene off at the Niedlich home for Amanda to see to her needs, Bill rushed Dorthea to the hospital. A couple of nurses attended to her, getting her situated. As she neared her delivery time the head nurse phoned Dr. Keller.

He hurried himself to the hospital. Everyone went about their normal activities, except Bill, of course. Pacing the corridors seemed to be his mode for the time being, not sure that he wanted to go through this experience again. Twice was enough, he felt.

In minutes past two hours of labor time, Frederick William Beck was born. He was named after his Uncle Fritz, Dorthea's brother, and after his father.

Bill went in to see the mother of his son, folding her in his arms, he said, "You did a fine job, Dorthea, Thank you for our son."

They were both happy, and also thankful that all had gone well.

The next day Amanda dropped the girls off at the grandparents, and went to see this new wonder. He was a big baby, weighing in at eight pounds. Amanda held him and cooed to him, then handed him back to his mother.

"You'll be his baptismal sponsor, Amanda, won't you?"

"Of course I will!" she eagerly offered.

They visited on and Amanda had the pleasure of holding her new godchild one more time before she left.

Time went on and between school, gardening and preparing for the wedding, Tamar was kept very busy. On Saturday, after the cleaning and baking, Amanda suggested that she and Tamar take some of the cookies that they had just baked, over to their neighbor, Loretta. She felt that it was about time to get better acquainted with her. But for all of her busyness, Tamar hesitated, then acquiesced. Taking Ruth with them they walked over, talking about the great injustice the town's people had imposed upon Loretta.

Answering the door, Loretta welcomed them in.

Amanda introduced herself and said, "We won't keep you from your work. We just wanted to say 'Hello' and bring you some cookies we just baked."

Loretta accepted the gift and spoke to Ruth. Ruth voiced her greeting.

Amanda said, "This is my oldest daughter, Tamar."

"I'm pleased to meet you, Tamar."

Adding only a few more sentences they left, knowing that their work at home was still waiting for them.

On the walk home Amanda voiced, "Well, that makes me feel a lot better."

"It was a great gesture, Mom," Tamar replied.

They arrived home. Amanda's heart felt a lot lighter and they finished their work with good timing.

Vivian's sufferance of two and a half weeks was up. Driving herself to Timothy's office, she was anticipating life without the cast and crutches. Again, she looked stunning in a blue crepe dress with white piping.

As Timothy entered the small room where Vivian was seated on the examining table, his heart palpitated at her winsome smile.

"You look like you're ready to take on the whole world," he voiced.

"I'm ready," she replied.

"Well let's see if we can get you there."

They chatted a bit as he sawed at the cast. He was very impressed with this young woman. Vivian felt a certain pull towards him, too.

The cast having been removed, Timothy checked her foot and ankle.

"You're ready," he announced.

Hating to see her go, he chatted some more and as she was leaving said, "I need some reading material. I'll probably see you soon."

Vivian was delighted with that statement. She thought Timothy very nice looking and a fine gentleman.

The next Sunday the Ladies Aid had organized a bridal shower for Tamar and Paul. This took place after church, starting with a potluck. Children and men were also invited. After the meal the men played ball, some visited and some played croquet. The woman played bridal games, subtly teasing Tamar, and then she opened her gifts. Paul and Tamar were overwhelmed by the outpouring of such beautiful gifts. There were bathroom towels, kitchen towels, cooking utensils and more. Some of the members had gone together and purchased a place setting for twelve, of good dishes for them. A set of silverware came from Tamar's aunts and uncles and grandparents. Amanda and Herb had surprised them with

matching end tables for their living room. Timothy, who was to be the groomsman, presented them with money for their honeymoon. The best man and his family gave them a Silex coffee percolator, a two-pound can of coffee and a set of six cups with pretty plates, for their coffee entertaining. Even though the war was over, coffee was still a bit hard to come by. Martin was aware that they both liked their coffee. Paul and Tamar were very grateful and they both voiced their gratitude, Paul doing most of it since he was the orator of the family-to-be.

In closing they sang the song, "Bless Be The Tie That Binds." Immediately thereafter, Paul and Tamar, with help from the relatives, the best man and the groomsman, toted all the things to the parsonage. Paul offered his thanks again and they all left, leaving the couple to their own relevance.

Paul immediately hugged Tamar. "Where will we put all these things!"

"Just wait and see. We'll find room for them." Tamar's answer was positive.

They started putting things away, as best they could; at least until Tamar had a chance to delve into it with more time on her hands. The end tables were put to use immediately. The two unmatched end tables that Paul had been using, were placed in one of the upstairs bedrooms where they could be used at a later time. Tamar did take time to wash the set of dishes, Paul drying them for her, and placed them in their new home in the cupboard that she had recently cleaned.

It was time to get Tamar back to St. Paul. This would be her last week of school.

Their wedding day was closing in on them.

On Friday when Paul went to pick up Tamar, they went to a jewelry store to pick out their wedding rings. Tamar was very excited, butterflies fluttering about in her stomach. Soon she'd be amongst the wedded population. She was a bit apprehensive, though. Perhaps her role wouldn't be as smooth as she had anticipated. She had been praying that she would make a good wife for Paul and that she would adhere to her Christian duties as Paul's wife with steadfast endurance. She would continue her prayers.

They chose their rings.

That evening the school band was playing in the park and Paul and Tamar were amongst those who were listening. He wanted to hold her hand but with a crowd of people around, he sacrificed. Inasmuch, he had his position to consider, although he was sure that God would not mind. After all, God had created man and woman to be together. To hold her hand would be a pleasure. It was what he would cause others to think that made him reconsider. He would not be party to giving their tongues something to talk about. A chance to hold her hand would avail itself as he drove Tamar home.

Rose and Joe happened along and sat with them. The music was delightful, the weather was excellent and the company heart warming.

On Saturday evening, Paul had supper with the Niedlich family, and stayed after for the "singsperation."

Bill and Dorthea came with the new baby. Everyone wanted a turn holding him.

Paul talked with Dorene and asked her how she liked her new brother.

"He's mine and you can't have him," she answered.

"Can I hold him?"

Dorene looked at her mother.

Dorthea said, "It's okay if he holds him, Dorene. He won't hurt him."

Paul picked up Freddy and talked to him softly.

Laughing, Dorthea said, "You look good with babies in your arm, Paul."

"Hopefully, God will grant us a good many," he said as he winked at Tamar.

Tamar blushed and said, "Wait a minute. Don't I have a say in all of this?"

Paul laughed and said, "I'm only teasing, Tamar." He winked again.

Freddy was a good baby and slept most of the evening.

They went on with their singing. Tamar played a few songs, eager to run the keyboard again. Their voices could be heard up and down the street.

Paul left right after Amanda had served cake and coffee, knowing that he needed to be well rested for the service the next day.

As Tamar went to bed that night, she reflected on the weekend. It would be strange not going back to school. She had hoped to go back in the fall but time would tell if that would be a factor. She thought about what Rose had told her at the park. Rumors were around that Maxine was very unhappy in her marriage. Tamar felt sorry for her. A prayer was in order for Maxine, and Tamar did remember to include her along with her prayers.

Maxine had been home staying with her folks for a week. Lawrence had finally gone to talk things over with her and had taken her back home in Mankato. She wanted to open a beauty shop in Mankato and Lawrence hoped that she would just want to be a housewife. He finally relented. Thus was the rumor.

Timothy found time on Monday afternoon, to go to the library for some reading material. Vivian, checking in some books, looked up at him with her usual cheery smile, and graciously received him. She helped Timothy find the section of books that he was interested in. Taking time to chat with her, again he was smitten. They seemed to have an abundance of things to talk about, which prompted Timothy to ask her to dine with him that evening. She accepted.

Now that school was behind her, Tamar took time to put all of the gifts in their rightful places at the parsonage. Wedding details were also attended too. She was full of anticipation, awe and a bit apprehensive too. *Will I make a good minister's wife?* she asked herself. *I'll always pray that I follow God's leading,* was her final assessment.

Chapter Twenty-seven

The wedding day that God had created for Paul and Tamar was gorgeous. Tamar knew that it was the perfect day. She, in her bedroom, and Paul in his, each in their own way, praised their Heavenly Father for the beautiful gift of this day and for their soon-to-be mate.

Paul was a bit electrified as he hurried through his morning devotions. He had to stay centered though, there was a service for him to conduct this morning. The wedding would take place at 2:00 this afternoon.

Mrs. Riech, Paul's mother, had arrived on Saturday, and was getting breakfast ready. She was an island of calm.

Paul's sister, expecting another baby at any minute, was disappointed that she would not be able to attend this joyous day in her brother's life. She remembered them in prayer.

Tamar was more than electrified. She was full of jitters. Her heart intoned to her mind that all would go well, but her mind wouldn't cooperate. She knew, though, that she had chosen a good life with Paul. God would help her iron out the rough and flimsy areas, she was certain. Hurrying along with the day, she went downstairs.

The organist, Martha Hinrichs, from Spruce Island, arrived at the church just before 1:30. Walking down the aisle she noted the beauty of the church. White carnations and white, satin ribbons had been attached to each pew. No white carpet would decorate this aisle. Tamar chose to save the money instead. The altar area was filled with flowers. Bridal wreath from Dorthea's and the Niedlich's bushes, and white peonies from their neighbor's yard, along with fern, had been placed in beautiful

containers. It looked like a radiant garden. All was in readiness. She walked to the organ and laid out her music. She'd have time to practice a bit before anyone else arrived.

Music floating through the windows of St. Peters was enthralling as Paul arrived at the church with his mother. He closed himself in his office, knelt before his Master and poured out his heart to Him. In closeness with his Maker, he knew that his life lay in the hands of his Master. With Him all things were possible. Paul finished with his communication, and took care of last minute details on his desk. Soon he gathered with his entourage, Martin, Timothy and Tamar's cousin, Robert Platz, who was the ring bearer.

Tamar, nervously excited, was in the basement getting dressed for this blessed event. She had said her prayers, praying that all would go well. Amanda and Dorthea were in the basement helping her get ready.

The Reverend Sprode from St. Paul's, in Spruce Island, had been commissioned to do the honors.

Paul was ready and waiting for the nuptial to commence. Assembling near the altar, he watched for the bride to appear with her father.

Amanda kissed her daughter and said, "You are a beautiful bride, Tamar. It's time to begin."

Dorthea hugged Tamar and then went to sit with her family.

Tamar was fearfully and wonderfully anxious as Amanda led her to Herb. Herb smiled at her, but underneath that smile Tamar saw a few tears gathering.

John, one of the ushers, escorted his mother, Amanda, to her seat.

The Bridal March began and the maid of honor and bridesmaid started down the aisle. The flower girl, Ruth, walking behind them, was tossing rose pedals along the aisle, enjoying every minute of it. When she got to the aisle where her Uncle Bill, Aunt Dorthea with the baby, and Dorene were sitting, she threw some at Dorene. A few chuckles erupted from those who witnessed the playful gesture.

Paul, although by nature a calm individual, was rocking from one foot to the other. Then he noticed Tamar ready to walk down the aisle. Although beads of perspiration had gathered on his forehead, and his

palms were sweaty, he broke into a charming smile.

Walking towards her love, Tamar, making contact with his eyes and with a rapturous look, smiled her prettiest. Their hearts at that moment were divinely entwined.

Her dress was beautiful with a small train flowing behind. Her veil was a borrowed item from Rose. She carried a bouquet of white roses along with white satin streamers, that were artistically designed around her white Bible.

Herb, two-stepped her to Paul who eagerly turned and crooked his arm for her. They beheld the minister. Paul, in his navy blue suit, a boutonniere in his lapel, with a necktie in shades of blue, stood six inches above Tamar. Even so, they were a nice looking couple.

The ceremony continued and Herb answered wistfully, at the right moment, that he and Amanda gave Tamar to Paul. Then wiping tears from his eyes, he observed that his daughter was a beautiful bride, and he prayed that Paul would always take care of her. He thought, *there's nothing else that I can do for her now but pray. From now on it's up to Paul. How did she grow up so fast?*

The wedding ritual over with, Paul and Tamar, with her hand in the crook of his arm, smiled widely at the audience. Walking towards the back of the church, Paul nodded at them as they strolled along. Tamar just smiled.

Greetings, hugs and kisses over with, the couple assembled in the basement for the rest of the celebration.

All went well, gifts on the table were forced to spill over onto the floor for lack of space. Wishes were on going, and then it was time to throw the bouquet. Tamar removed her Bible from the roses and streamers, and eagerly tossed the fragrant bouquet, which landed in her Aunt Margie's hands. Everyone cheered.

After a few more handshakes the couple left for their honeymoon in Milwaukee.

Paul drove away from the church and when they were out of sight, stopped and drew Tamar towards him, giving her a sweet, lingering kiss, and said, "I'm so very happy that God made you and equally happy that He gave you to me."

"And you are finally mine. God in His goodness gave you to me. How great God is!" They sealed their declaration with another kiss.

A journey into married life lay ahead of them. What fears, heartaches and happiness it contained only God, their Father knew. Paul was sure of one thing, that with God at the helm of their ship, he need not fear. He would trust all to him. He looked forward, in awe and reverence, to their future.

Tamar thought, *Paul is the polished arrow. I'm but the bow. But one is useless without the other. We must work together. However, there is a more significant paramount. Without Jesus neither one of us will be able to do a flourishing ministry for Him. He is the key, the One that will release the arrow from the bow. Paul and I need to work together with Christ. Paul has a special gift given to him by our Father. What an awesome and fearful journey we are just beginning!*

They drove off into the sunset, a sunset that was but a beginning—a oneness, a total togetherness as God had ordained.

The End

Printed in the United States
21751LVS00004B/283